LABYRINTH

LABYRINTH

DIANE STEVENS

DOUBLEDAY & COMPANY, INC., GARDEN CITY, NEW YORK 1976

All of the characters in this book
are fictitious, and any resemblance
to actual persons, living or dead,
is purely coincidental.

Library of Congress Cataloging in Publication Data

Stevens, Diane.
Labyrinth.

I. Title.
PZ4.S8439Lab [PS3569.T4512]   813'.5'4
ISBN 0-385-12201-2
Library of Congress Catalog Card Number 76–2821

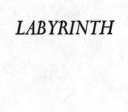

LABYRINTH

CHAPTER 1

Castle Cabot was still imposing, if a bit gloomy, in the dappled moonlight. I leaned back against the tree, hidden from casual glances by the shadows, and stared at the outlines of the big house, its muted golden rectangles of light even now beckoning to me with all its old fascination. The red house with its gray slate roofs, seven brick chimneys and its copper-plated turrets was imprinted on my memory. Once, in my fantasies, I had pictured myself as the chatelaine of Castle Cabot—Bruce's wife. But I had thrown all that away, and when I fled Kingsville I had tried to put it behind me.

To a large extent I had been successful. I had fallen into a challenging job and had immersed myself in it. My zeal had paid off in promotions, and now I was an assistant administrator at San Francisco's International Airport. The job took up most of my time; there were always emergencies to be dealt with, people to placate. When I wasn't working I went to night school and on weekends to a whirl of parties, concerts and movies.

I had had no intention of ever returning to Kingsville. Even when I had received Paul Darcey's first letter eight months ago and learned that my father had disappeared more than two years before, I hadn't considered coming back. My father and I had never been close. He was a quiet, often secretive man. We seldom talked. At times I wouldn't see him for days. I had always thought that his neglect was because I reminded him too much of my mother who had died when I was ten. After her death he had hired someone to look after me, and then I had fallen into the habit of taking care of myself. The news of his disappearance and presumed death saddened me a little, but I saw no reason to return.

The second letter had come four months later. This time Paul Darcey had written telling me of the opportunity to sell some property my father had owned to a group interested in building a ski resort on the west slope of the Colorado Rockies. I should have written and told him to get the best price he could, but I had been intrigued by the revelation that my father, whom I had always thought of simply as King Cabot's mine foreman, had owned land along Cottonwood Creek, one of the several side canyons that cut into the Kingsville Box. It had never occurred to me that he possessed anything more than the small frame miner's house in which I had grown up.

This unexpected knowledge teased my curiosity. I was at a loss to know how my father had obtained the property for he had never had much money. In fact, the money for my two years of college had been borrowed from King Cabot. I left Paul Darcey's letters unanswered until, finally, in a moment of sudden decision, I flew to Albuquerque, rented a car and drove north to Colorado through the piñon pines and mesquite of the mesa country and into the crumpled mass of the San Juan Mountains.

The walls of the Kingsville Box were black hulks against the nighttime sky. I slapped at a mosquito that had been buzzing around my face, and the sound echoed in the still alpine air. A light went on in one of the upstairs rooms of the Castle. I could see a figure silhouetted against the window, and I wondered if it was Bruce.

I had admired Bruce Cabot from childhood. We had grown up together, along with his twin sister, Lynn, and his older half-brother, Geoffrey. Until the summer I was nineteen Bruce had always treated me as a friend; a playmate when we were young and then a casual companion. I don't know why he noticed me that summer for I hadn't changed. All my life I had suffered under the double burden of being plain and intelligent. My teenage years had been a dreary succession of half-suppressed longings and empty daydreams, and although Bruce had his place in them, so did most everyone else, even on rare occasions Geoffrey.

For some reason Bruce picked me as his girl that summer. Perhaps he was bored with pretty faces. Perhaps because I had been away at college he suddenly looked at me differently. I reveled in his attention and fell in love with him. I told myself that he reciprocated my feelings. Afterward, when it was over, filled with self-pity, I blamed Bruce. He had been playing with me I decided, and it was inevitable that he would turn from me to someone more glamorous. Other times I was much harder on myself, unable to escape the knowledge that my insecurity, possessiveness and demands had driven him away as much as Carole had lured him away. As is so often the case, the truth was probably somewhere in between.

Carole was beautiful. Blond, with pale blue eyes and a stunning figure, she was the type of girl who drew everyone's attention. She had come to Kingsville on a vacation and had stayed to become the princess of Castle Cabot. Her first target had been Geoffrey Cabot, who was taciturn and withdrawn and generally didn't give anyone more than a casual glance. Lynn maintained that this had sparked Bruce's interest. Whatever the cause, before I knew it we were all plunged into a tangled web of deceit, anger and, of course, pain. I didn't have the self-confidence necessary to give Bruce his head. His interest in Carole only accentuated my insecurity. I pleaded. I begged. I stormed and threw tearful tantrums. Then one day Lynn came down from the Castle to tell me that Bruce and Carole had eloped. I was numb with the pain of betrayal and rejection. I left Kingsville then.

Over the years in San Francisco I had grown, matured, gained a better sense of myself and had come to see the events of that summer with a degree of perspective. But perspective didn't alter the pain, nor did it erase the scar on my personality. Carefully, I rebuilt my shattered shell and, turtlelike, carried it with me. They say that scar tissue is stronger than the original tissue, but I had never tested mine.

Now I had come back to Kingsville. I knew that while I was curious about my father's property, it wasn't the only reason for my return. I was twenty-nine. I had brooded over Bruce Cabot for too many years, and I was plagued by the knowledge that I should at last see him with adult eyes. Perhaps then I would finally rid myself of the past and get on with the business of living.

The next morning I got my first look at Kingsville in ten years. It was an ordinary little town, no different from any other mining town in Colorado that had grown too fast and was gradually having to retrench as the mines became consolidated and mechanized. It looked sleepy in the morning sun—wood-frame houses, many with paint peeling, a few brick structures, many of them abandoned. The town nestled in the floor of the valley and then rose along the hillsides like a bizarre crop of trees.

Kingsville was in a narrow, glacier-shaped valley, high in the San Juan Mountains. The valley ended in a box canyon about five miles from the town. The big mill of the Colvada Mining Company with its gray-yellow tailings ponds lay between Kingsville and Castle Cabot. The Castle sat at the head of the Box, perched precariously on a narrow bench at the base of the 2,000-foot escarpment. Part of the Castle was hewn out of the rock of the cliff, the rest was built of the reddish, orthoclase-flecked granite that dominated the geology of the region. The escarpment rose behind the Castle—shear, almost impregnable except for the narrow, twisting, hairpin jeep road that laboriously wound its way to the top and disappeared into Mithral Basin, gradually losing itself in the maze of the San Juans.

On either side of the Castle two sparkling waterfalls dropped down the cliff, looking at this distance like two gossamer threads in a Japanese silk screen. A smile crossed my lips as I remembered soaking my feet in the cool pools at the bottom of the falls, getting sprayed by the fine mist. I'd forgotten how much I loved this high, hanging Colorado valley; how much I had missed it during all the frenetic years in San Francisco. I would have to visit the falls, I resolved, after I had seen my father's lawyer.

Although Paul Darcey had come to Kingsville during my long absence, I found his office easily. In a town the size of Kingsville it wasn't hard to drive down the main street and see the small, neatly lettered sign. I parked and walked determinedly into the small building. The outer office was neat and sparse—a few filing cabinets, several topographic maps of the Kingsville quadrangle on the wall, a desk and a typewriter. The girl looked up as I swung the door open and waited for me to say something.

"I'd like to see Mr. Darcey if it's possible," I said.

She looked somewhat dubious, although I thought to myself that while Paul Darcey might be out fishing, he was certainly not overrun with clients. And it was no wonder. Who needed a lawyer up here?

"Well . . ." She hesitated as though she had never before been confronted with this kind of situation. "What's your name?"

"Jenifer Trent," I told her.

She wrote the name down, as if to make sure that she remembered it, and disappeared through a door at the rear of the room. The door opened again and a tall, thin man with tousled brown hair, steady brown eyes and a warm smile strode out.

"Miss Trent." He extended his hand toward the open door. "Please come in. This is an unexpected pleasure." Despite his words I had the feeling he had been expecting me.

I smiled at him, walked into his office and sat down on one of the two chairs obviously meant for clients and visitors. Again, the office was sparsely furnished. There were several bookcases of law books at the far end of the room. His law diploma was hanging on the wall, and there were a few photographs of the Box and the surrounding San Juans. The desk was slightly messy, and I had the fleeting impression that he arranged it deliberately in order to make himself think that he had something to do. There was a picture of a grim-faced auburn-haired woman on the desk. It had been years and she had changed, but I recognized Lynn Cabot immediately.

Paul Darcey lowered his long body into his old red-leather chair and stared at me for a moment. "I had begun to despair of ever hearing from you. I thought perhaps we had found the wrong Jenifer Trent. It took us a long time to track you down. No one seemed to know your whereabouts after you left here. I assume you received my letters about your father's presumed death and disposing of your property."

"Yes, I got your letters. I apologize for not answering them. I decided it would be best to come back and deal with these matters personally. I'm not entirely clear about what happened to my father. Perhaps we could start there."

He made a tent out of his fingers and nervously tapped them together. "It was . . . a little over three years ago now, about this time of year. John had a meeting with King Cabot one afternoon but didn't show up. When King started looking for him, he found his jeep up in Mithral Basin, but there was no sign of John. We sent out search parties; King even had dogs brought in from Denver, but they never found a trace. He just disappeared. We've always assumed that he must have had an accident somewhere in the San Juans. No one had seen him for several days before he was due to see King, so we were never able to pinpoint when he left the jeep or where he might have gone."

He stopped his recital and looked at me as if he were trying to judge my reaction.

"I assumed from your letters that my father's will leaves everything to me."

He settled back in his chair and looked more comfortable. "Yes. The terms of the will are basically simple," he told me in a casual, yet businesslike way. "Your father made you the heir, if you were still alive. If not, he stipulated that everything was to go to Geoffrey Cabot."

Geoffrey Cabot! I kept my face impassive but I was astounded. Since I hadn't communicated with my father after I'd left Kingsville, I could see why he might make a provision for the disposal of the property in case I were dead or couldn't be located, but Geoffrey Cabot was a strange choice.

"What precisely does his estate consist of besides the house and this property on Cottonwood Creek?" I asked him.

He looked at me closely. Picking up a letter opener he started playing with it. "There's the house and the property, as you say. Then there are several thousand shares of Cabot stock—" He broke off, noticing my blank look.

"Cabot stock?"

"Yes. Some years ago King Cabot made the Colvada Mining Company into a private corporation and issued shares of stock. The move was really for tax purposes. Most of the stock—all of it as a matter of fact—is held by the Cabot family, except for the shares your father owned."

"How much is the stock worth?"

"Present market value, I'd say about thirty thousand dollars," Paul Darcey said cheerfully. "Of course, the metals market has been uncertain of late."

Thirty thousand dollars. Property. I was astonished. I had, it seemed, known very little about my father.

"Then there's a small sum of money. About a thousand dollars after some small legal expenses and paying property taxes for three years. I'd be glad to show you the records if you like. There are two rather large gold pieces, and there is a lockbox that has never been opened. None of us have the keys. Not knowing what might be inside, I took the liberty of putting it in the bank for safe keeping. If you don't have the keys, we can force it open."

I had the feeling that Paul Darcey was waiting for me to respond. When I said nothing, he tossed the letter opener on the desk and continued heartily. "These days it's not a great deal of money, but then again it's not a paltry sum either. Land values are tremendously inflated since the skiing people have decided to come in. If you'll agree to sell the Cottonwood property, I think that you can assure yourself of an estate in the neighborhood of a quarter of a million dollars.

"Under Colorado law, of course, you can't take possession of the estate for four more years since your father's body was never recovered, and so there's no actual proof that he's deceased. Ordinarily, in cases like this, we'd have to go into court and have you named as the guardian of the estate so that we could sell the property. Fortunately, however, several months before he disappeared, John had given me the general power of attorney, which means that I can act in his name until he's legally declared dead and you come into the estate."

I refused to give him the satisfaction of voicing amazement. I stared at him, using a penetrating look I'd found particularly useful for impressing people and getting information out of them at the same time. He returned the look, and I could see his brown eyes narrowing thoughtfully for just a moment before he broke off to smile at me. His casual appearance was deceptive, I decided. He was a very careful man.

"I don't know if I'll want to sell the property," I said calmly. "I want to see it first. I'm not clear about exactly where it is."

"Of course you'll want to see it and to meet the gentlemen who propose to buy it. I can take you up there at your convenience and then arrange a meeting with Dan Greenberg." There was a pause. "Are you going to be in Kingsville long?" He asked the question suddenly, as though he hoped to catch me off guard. I wondered why.

I opened my purse and extracted a cigarette, lit it and blew a stream of smoke into the air between us before I answered. "Perhaps," I told him. "I haven't made definite plans." I changed the subject. "I'd like to see the deed and other papers relating to the property."

He nodded. "They're on file in the county courthouse in Telluride. I think you'll find, however, that the title papers are rather unsatisfactory. The land was homesteaded by Dick McGuire in 1879. After his death the title is blank until your father recorded his deed. There's nothing that indicates how he came into possession of it. It's rather unusual," he added significantly, "but there's no doubt that the property is yours to dispose of as you wish."

He had answered part of my question without my asking. It reinforced my vague suspicions that my father had come into possession of the land in a questionable manner. I wondered how I could find out how he had gotten it. Perhaps a search of his house would turn something up. Then there was the lockbox Paul Darcey had mentioned.

I stubbed the cigarette out in the ash tray on the desk. "I'd like to look at my father's house. Perhaps you could give me the key. I'll go over there later on. I shall take you up on your offer to show me the property, but not today. I want to get reacquainted with Kingsville. Tomorrow perhaps." I stood up, giving him my broadest smile. I wanted to digest the information he had given me before I talked to him any further. I had the sudden feeling that I was poised above a pool of quicksand, and I needed time to think.

He made me wait for a moment. Then he opened his desk drawer, took out a key chain with a big skeleton key dangling from it, and handed it to me. I glanced at the piece of tape that was wrapped around the medallion. It bore my father's name— John Trent.

I moved toward the door. "Thank you for your time and patience. You've been very helpful." I left him then, hoping that he was intrigued and puzzled by me. Once I had seen Lynn's picture on his desk, I had known that he would report to the Cabots.

I drove along the far side of the tailings on an old, little-used back road. Parking on a widened shoulder usually used by fishermen, I quickly found the path that would take me to the top of Rob Roy Falls, the waterfall that plummeted down the right side of the Kingsville escarpment. It was a steep, breathless climb of about a thousand feet, and despite my long indoor city life, I reached the top in half an hour, proud of myself for being only a little winded. The path had been overgrown in spots, and I could tell that few people used it these days.

The view was as breathtaking as I remembered. Rob Roy Basin opened up immediately behind the falls. It was late July, and by this time of the year the Basin had lost most of its snow and was covered with velvet-green grass, ablaze with wild flowers. Snow still lay, however, on the highest peaks of the San Juans.

I gazed up the Basin picking out the old dumps, glacial moraines and the sink ponds filled with icy snow water, noting absently the characteristic U-shape of the glacier-formed terrain. Halfway up the Basin were the massive ruins of the Rob Roy Mine. Many times Lynn and I had played there, often joined by Bruce.

It was said that the Rob Roy was the largest of all the hundreds of abandoned mines in the San Juans. The dumps spread from one side of the Basin to the other like some prehistoric dam, washed in places where the creek had cut through the sand and loose rocks. Old buildings with fallen roofs, tar paper peeling off the sides, dotted the dumps; the towers and cable from the tramway lay toppled and rusty at odd intervals. Slightly behind me, at the edge of Rob Roy Falls, was an old tramway stop. The two-story building leaned a bit to one side, its weathered boards telling of harsh winters and bitter winds. Huge chunks of tar paper lay in heaps on the ground. An occasional badly rusted piece of machinery added to the austere litter around the building. The cable that had connected this part of the tramway with the hoist in the floor of the Box was still intact. It hung suspended in the clear Colorado air like a giant tightrope, plunging at a steep angle over a beautiful green and brown and red abyss.

I glanced at the big white-and-red sign posted on the side of the building, next to the door which hung crookedly, half off its hinges. "Colvada Mining Company," it read, "Private Property. Dangerous. Keep Out."

I walked upstream for a bit and then found a rock to sit on. I trailed my hand in the cold water while I tried to collect my thoughts. My meeting with Paul Darcey had left me puzzled.

I had sensed very early in my life that my father was obsessed by the mines. For a long while he would work at the Colvada mill until late evening. Then he began making furtive trips in the middle of the night, taking his miner's lamp, geologist's pick and sample sacks with him. Sometimes he carried a full sample sack when he came back; other times he came back empty-handed. Occasionally, he would disappear for several days at a time. I soon got used to his eccentricities. I was curious, but I never dwelt on it; I was too wrapped up in my own problems.

But now, these unexpected legacies led me back to consider his behavior. Where had he gone on those dark trips, and what had he been looking for? A strike on Cottonwood Creek? I wondered. It was possible, except that everyone knew there was nothing of value on the creek. The question of how and why he had gotten the land still nagged at my mind. Instinctively, I sensed that something was not right about the whole affair.

Then there was the curious fact of his stipulation in the will about Geoffrey Cabot. As far as I knew, Father and Geoffrey had never been close. It was puzzling enough, although explainable, why he had felt it necessary to name an alternate heir, but I couldn't think of any reason why he would pick Geoffrey.

The strangest part, however, was why he had given Paul Darcey his power of attorney. Had he intended to disappear, I wondered? People did such things I knew—vanished to start new lives in Australia or Argentina. Before this morning I had accepted Father's disappearance; now I began to wonder what had happened to him and how I could possibly find out.

I splashed at the water and sighed softly to myself. It was impossible to come to any conclusion at this point. I needed more information. I sensed that I would have to delve, like a seeker for gold or silver, trying to unearth it.

I leaned over to drink from the stream. I was looking back toward the crest of Rob Roy Falls. The timber line began in a stand of stunted pine trees about half a mile from my vantage point. Darting along the edge of the trees, I saw a horse and rider. He crouched low over the saddle, dodging among the uneven line of pines. I could hear the dull thud of the horse's hooves. I stood up, straining to see against the bright Western sun, but by this time the rider had disappeared. He was some horseman, I marveled, for to get down to the floor of the Box from the point at which I had last seen him, he would have had to descend the narrow rocky path I had used.

Disconcerted somewhat by the fact that I wasn't alone, I was nonetheless thankful that I had been saved the task of explaining who I was and how I had come up here. I was still staring at the ragged line of trees when I heard the rifle shot. Automatically, I connected it with the rider I had seen, and idly wondered what he had been shooting at.

I picked up a small rock and heaved it into the stream, watching the water splash and then ripple around it. Slowly, I walked back to the Falls. The sun was warm, so I decided to lie on one of the rocks and bask in it. I was ruefully white. I shed my windbreaker and my shoes, rolled up my jeans, and stretched myself on the flattest rock I could find. I dozed a while, listening to the sounds of the water rushing over the precipice, trying to empty my mind and relax. After all, I reasoned, this was my vacation. Even if there were some unanswered questions about my father, and even though I had yet to see Bruce Cabot again, I might as well enjoy myself.

I didn't know how long I had slept when I became aware that the sun was no longer as warm as it had been. I yawned and looked at my watch. Amazingly, I had been here only an hour. It had seemed much longer.

When I sat up, I saw him.

He was across the stream from me, and he must have come from the trees where I had seen the rider. He was staring at me intently with a serious, almost grim expression on his face. He must have been all of nine, a slight boy with dark hair.

I smiled at him. "Hello. Have you been there long?"

He stared at me, saying nothing.

I tried again. "I must have fallen asleep in the sun. Are you from around here?"

Again he didn't answer.

I started putting my tennis shoes on while I continued talking to him. "I always liked to come up here. It's very peaceful. You can sit and listen to the water, and you're so far above the town that it almost doesn't seem to exist."

I tied the last knot in my shoelace and tilted my head back to look up at what an hour before had been a clear blue sky. Now clouds had drifted in. Above me they were white, billowy thunderheads, while over the San Juans behind me, they were angry and black.

"I think it's going to rain." It was like talking to myself. So far the boy hadn't moved. He just stood there, staring at me with a wide, unblinking gaze.

Methodically, I rolled down my jeans and stood up to put on my windbreaker. One more time I told myself. "I thought I'd be alone up here, but a little while ago there was a rider in those woods and now you. Rob Roy seems to be popular this morning."

At that he seemed to come alive. Carefully, he began to cross the stream. I watched him closely because the rocks were slippery and a wrong step could send him over the brink of the falls. He was surefooted though, as if he had accomplished this journey many times. Soon he stood in front of me, still looking at me with that serious, half-grim gaze.

"Then you saw him too?" he asked me. His voice was grave for a child, and now that he was near me I could see that his blue eyes were somber and veiled as if he were keeping something hidden. This was no ordinary little boy.

"The man on horseback? Yes, I saw him, but I don't know who it was. I was up at the bend of the creek looking at the Rob Roy and couldn't see very well."

He seemed relieved. "Oh." He paused for a moment and then went on. "It's nice up here. I like this waterfall better than the other one." It was the smallest of polite small talk. Still, I was gratified that he now seemed willing to converse.

He hadn't looked at me since he had begun speaking. Suddenly, his long lashes flew up and he stared hard at me. "You're new here, aren't you?"

"In a way. I used to live here. My name's Jenifer Trent. What's yours?"

"Christopher," he replied, at last answering one of my questions. "I live down there." He nodded in the direction of the Castle.

"You mean Castle Cabot?" I asked, wanting to be sure.

He nodded a bit unhappily. He must be Bruce's son, I thought, looking at him with renewed interest.

"Then you're a Cabot. I used to know your father. Bruce and your Aunt Lynn and I sort of grew up together." I gave him my most winning smile. For some reason I wanted him to like me.

His blue eyes were ice. *"He's* not my father!"

I was bewildered. "He's not?" I echoed stupidly. "I'm terribly sorry." I peered at him. I didn't know why I had not noticed the resemblance at once. He had the same blue eyes, dark hair and aloofness. "You mean Geoffrey is your father?"

He nodded abruptly.

"I really am sorry," I apologized once more. I wanted to ask why he disliked Bruce so, but I didn't want to frighten him and I sensed that this was a tender subject. "I left Kingsville a long time ago, and I didn't know Geoff had gotten married."

"Yes, I know," he said, relenting a bit. "I heard them talking about you. Are you still in love with Uncle Bruce?" He asked the question that abrupt, frank way that children have.

I laughed nervously. I hadn't expected my first hurdle to come from a boy. "Good heavens. I haven't seen him in ten years."

"They're going to invite you up for dinner. Aunt Lynn went down to find you."

"Well, in that case I'll be seeing you again, won't I?"

"I guess so," he replied.

We looked at one another for a moment. I smiled at him, but couldn't get him to break out of his seriousness. My heart ached for him. He was far too young to be so grave. Apparently Geoffrey's wife was as silent and taciturn as he.

A sudden crack of thunder shook the sky above us, reverberating and echoing around the Basin. I looked up to see that the black rain clouds had moved rapidly; they were almost upon us.

"It's going to storm. We had both better be going. I used the path over there. I suppose you came up the jeep road?"

He had become silent again and didn't answer my query.

"Well," I laughed, "I'm not in any mood to get drenched. If your information is correct, Christopher, I'll see you at dinner."

I started to move away but he caught my arm. As I turned to

look down at him, he whispered almost ominously. "Don't tell anyone you were up here today, or that you saw me."

He bolted past me then, running across the high Colorado meadow toward the jeep road.

I could only stare after him.

CHAPTER 2

The storm broke before I was halfway down the narrow, winding path. It was a hard, driving rain mixed with hail which pelted down, quickly making the rocks and brush shine. Within seconds I was soaked, my windbreaker proving to be no match for the Colorado tempest. Thunder roared at odd intervals. I picked my way carefully, not only because I knew the rocks underfoot were treacherously slick, but also because I was still somewhat preoccupied by my encounter with Christopher Cabot. He was a lonely, inner-directed boy, and I had the feeling that he was also very frightened about something. Of course, I reasoned, I could be making something out of nothing. Then I remembered his solemn tight face and his strange parting words. No. My instinctive feeling was correct. Geoffrey's son was not a normal, carefree boy.

I stopped for a moment and turned to look up at the blackened sky, closing my eyes as the rain streamed over my face. It was clean, this mountain rain. Wet as I was, it felt good.

I finally got back to the car, catching a glimpse of myself in the rear-view mirror as I got in. My hair was hanging in limp plaits, stuck close to my head. I looked very much like a drowned rat. I laughed at myself. I had a hard enough time trying to look attractive when I was dry. Thanking modern fashion for shag hair cuts and hot combs, I started the car and drove back to the hotel, still musing about Christopher.

Why, I wondered, didn't he want me to say that I had met him? Or even to say that I had been in the Basin? Then I remembered the black rider. Christopher had been unresponsive to my chatter until I mentioned seeing the rider; then he had come alive. Curious, I thought, and I wondered who the rider was.

———◆———

Angus MacDermott, an old-timer who ran Kingsville's only hotel, disengaged himself from the perpetual pan game in the hotel bar and came out to meet me as I started to climb the stairs. He had been in Kingsville as long as I could remember. Even in my childhood he had looked like a grizzled old prospector. Angus looked carefully at me and then at the small puddles of water my dripping clothes were leaving on the floor, but he said nothing.

"I got caught in the rain," I explained unnecessarily.

"Yep," he said noncommittally.

I had gone up several steps when he spoke again. "Lynn Cabot's been looking for you."

So Christopher had been right. "Thanks," I told him. He leaned against the newel post, watched me for a moment and then went back into the bar.

I had changed clothes, washed my hair and had a towel wrapped turban fashion around my head when I heard the knock on the door. Quickly, I toweled my hair a little drier before combing it. It still hung straight and damp, but it would have to do. Frowning at the streak of vanity that made me want to appear at my best, I crossed the room and opened the door.

"Hello, Lynn," I greeted her, smiling casually. "Come on in."

"Hi, Jenny." She kept her greeting terse. Her eyes swept over me, registering every detail of my appearance. I was sure she thought I looked terrible, and I would have to agree with her. She seemed to want to embrace me but settled instead for holding out her hand. It was shapely and well-tanned, with short, square-cut nails. She wore no rings but a narrow turquoise bracelet was clamped around her wrist. Glancing at her left hand, I saw a small diamond and wondered briefly if it was Paul Darcey's.

I shook her hand firmly. So strangers meet who were once friends.

On the surface, Lynn had changed little. She still had shoulder-length auburn hair and she carried herself with a kind of grace that was a characteristic of the Cabots. It was her face that was different. The picture in Paul Darcey's office had been an accurate one. She had a guarded, grave look. Her brown eyes didn't glimmer with fun anymore. Instead they were stony, serious.

"News travels fast it seems. I only arrived last night." I closed the door behind her as she walked into the room, glanced quickly around then leaned against the end of the bed.

She moved her hand impatiently. "You've forgotten a lot if you're surprised that everyone in Kingsville knows you're here. You should remember that everything is news in these backwater, rural towns. And no one ever forgets old news either," she finished significantly.

Noticing the wary look that crept into my face, she changed tack immediately. "I won't take up much of your time. I know you're probably busy taking care of your father's affairs. I came down to issue an invitation, actually. We'd like you to come up to the Castle for dinner tonight. Say about seven." It wasn't the most cordial invitation I'd ever received.

"We?"

She smiled, a bit ruefully I thought. "King and Elizabeth. You'll come?"

I could see Lynn watching me, trying to guess which way I was wavering, what I would say, preparing a rebuttal to my refusal. I smiled back at her and then, with as much warmth as I could muster, accepted. I could see that she was relieved not to have to argue with me.

She was quiet for a moment and then looked at me questioningly. "Have you changed, Jenny, or are you still the same?" It was an abrupt query and there was a terse steeliness behind it.

"Good heavens, Lynn," I laughed. "What kind of question is that? Everybody changes in ten years."

She turned away from me and walked to the small window,

pulled aside the thin, white cotton curtains and looked at the main street of Kingsville. I remained standing next to the dresser. I had no idea what would come next.

"You're right, of course. It was a stupid question." She turned back to me. "I suppose what I meant to say is that Bruce hasn't much. I always liked you, Jenny. You know that. I think Bruce made a poor choice. Just be careful." There was ice in her voice at the last.

Involuntarily, I shivered, and I knew my mouth was hanging open in amazement. I could think of no reply.

She started to say something else, then abruptly changed her mind. "I'll see you tonight." Then as an afterthought, "Elizabeth still requires that we dress for dinner." There was a note in her tone that I didn't begin to understand.

She strode to the door, opened it and turned slightly. "By the way. Welcome back." The words were right but there was no pleasure in her manner. She was gone then. I could hear her walking down the uncarpeted hallway, her heels rapping sharply against the board floor. In my mind's eye I could see her—lithe, slim and graceful.

I took out my hot comb, plugged it in and dried my hair. If Christopher had been strange, reserved and inexplicably grave, his aunt was even more so. Lynn had been the gay, frivolous one when we were growing up. Now, the brown eyes that I remembered dancing with excitement and mirth were still, while behind them flitted something else. It was hazy and ill-defined, as was everything since my return to Kingsville, but it was there. It saddened me.

Lynn had been a good friend. She had watched my affair with Bruce that summer with pity and understanding, unable to do anything to help me. I had loved her then. Something had changed her, and not for the better. I was beginning to get the idea that something was amiss with the Cabots.

My hair was dry now, brown and a bit fluffy. I grabbed a jacket, my sunglasses and my keys and ran down the stairs. As I left, I noticed that Angus was standing in the doorway leading to the bar, watching me. I would have to talk to Angus, I decided.

He could tell me some things I would need to know before I went to the Castle tonight.

In the meantime, I meant to search my father's house. I drove quickly through the dirt streets, until I was in front of a two-story, wood-frame house. The green paint had almost peeled off the sides of the house, and the shingles that I could see on the roof looked old and weary, tired of battling the elements.

The lock on the door was an old-fashioned variety. I had to jiggle the big skeleton key and twist the white porcelain knob several times before I could get it unlocked. The door swung open, hinges creaking. The small living room was mostly taken up by a large oil burner. Sheets covered the furniture. The narrow stairs to the second floor were jammed against the right-hand wall, one of the bedrooms opened off the living room and on my left, up one step, was the entrance to the kitchen. I sat on the lumpy sofa for a while, memories engulfing me. Then, rousing myself, I turned to the business at hand.

I pulled the sheets off into a heap on the floor and proceeded to systematically search everything, pulling out drawers, reading through stacks of old magazines and papers. It was a dusty business, but I kept at it.

After an hour I had found nothing but the remnants of my father's life. I decided that since the furniture was old and in fairly good condition I would try to sell it to the local antique dealer, and then I would list the house with a real estate agent. There was no sense in keeping it. I had no fond memories of it, only painful, lonely ones.

I had saved the mahogany desk until last in my search. It was a particularly handsome piece—tall, standing on lion's-paw legs, with drawers on the bottom half, glass-enclosed shelves on the top and a drop-down writing leaf which exposed a row of several very small drawers. Letter pigeonholes were above these surrounding a center compartment. They were filled with the usual desk items, stationery, envelopes, some old stamps, bottles of congealed glue and rolls of Scotch Tape.

I turned my attention to the center compartment. Two ornamental wooden pillars, perhaps two inches across and six inches high, were carved on either side of the small door. They stood out from the wood behind them. As my hand touched the wood, I felt it move.

Excited, I took hold of the thickest part of the pillar and began moving it from side to side. There was definitely something here. I pulled on the base of the pillar and a long, narrow section of the desk came out easily. Secret compartments, I thought wryly, and not very secret at that for anyone with half a knowledge of how these old desks were built.

I turned them both upside down. Nothing. They were too thin for my hand so I fished around with two fingers. The first one was empty. I sighed and turned my attention to the other. This time I could feel some paper. I found a pencil and continued to probe inside the small space, gradually working the paper toward the opening. After fifteen minutes, I had it.

It was an old envelope, yellowed with age. I opened it carefully. It cracked and split along the fold line. Two keys fell onto the desk. They were attached to a key chain which was run through a round piece of cardboard. The word "box" was written on it. One, I thought, must be the missing key to the lockbox. The other lay heavily in my hand. Two keys—or at least one—with no locks. It was time to talk to Angus.

———◆———

He was in the bar, playing pan. It was a common game in these small Western towns—a sort of variant of blackjack. I stood by the table waiting for a good moment to break in. Angus won the hand, and before he could deal I said quickly, "Angus, could I talk to you for a minute?"

He shuffled the cards several times, nodded his head and passed the deck to the next player. "Be back in a bit, boys. Have to take care of my paying customers." He chuckled to himself over that.

Angus MacDermott was a short, stocky, well-built man. With his full gray beard and leathery face, he looked like an old-time prospector. His eyes had almost disappeared in a mass of wrinkles, but occasionally I could see a glint of steel gray. He had heavy brows, which were still light brown, as was his hair. He was nearly seventy now, I guessed. He had lived in Kingsville ever since I could remember.

He led the way into his small cluttered office, sat down in a battered swivel chair and looked at me expectantly.

"I'd like to know about the Cabots. What's happened to them since I left?" I tried to ask the question casually, as though I were asking directions, which, in a strange way, I was. I knew, however, that Angus was shrewd enough to see beneath my attempted nonchalance.

Angus grinned. "Going up for dinner tonight, ain't you?"

For the second time that day I found myself saying, "News travels fast around here."

He stroked his beard. "Nope," he said shortly. "Not news. Lynn's pretty tight with information these days. But it don't take much to figure out what she come down here for."

I frowned thoughtfully. "Why is it so obvious that I would be invited to the Castle for dinner?"

"Nobody forgets around here, Jenifer," he told me cryptically.

I grimaced in annoyance. Lynn had said the same thing. "That's not a good enough explanation, Angus."

"You'll find out. King and Elizabeth both will want to size you up."

"But why? What have I to do with them?" I was beginning to get irritated.

"Everybody around here has to deal with the Cabots. You should know that."

I could feel his steel-gray eyes boring into me, even though I couldn't see them, and I knew what he was thinking. I had staked everything on my mad, passionate affair with Bruce Cabot, who had always been his mother's darling. And now I was back, and they would want to see if I had really just come to settle my father's estate or if I had come to make trouble. Yes, of course. I should have thought of it before.

"All right, Angus," I conceded. "But I do want some information. Is there something between Lynn and Paul Darcey?"

He was lighting his pipe. He drew on it for several moments

and then blew the match out, dropping it on the floor. "Wal," he drawled in an exaggerated manner. Angus was an intelligent, self-educated man, but often he chose to put on an illiterate, eccentric old-timer pose. I remembered from my childhood that Angus missed nothing, and having lived in Kingsville for half a century, he knew everything. "They've been 'engaged,'" he emphasized the word slightly, "three, maybe four years."

"And they haven't gotten married?"

"Nope."

I waited a moment, but he didn't elaborate. Getting answers from Angus, even to obvious questions, was a task. "Why not?" Then acidly, "Angus, you certainly could be a little more helpful."

"Yep," he agreed cheerfully. "I could. And then on the other hand, all I got's my opinions. Who knows why they never got married except them. And mebbe they don't even know."

He was right. I dropped the subject. "How about Geoffrey?"

"Geoffrey. He got married." Angus took the pipe out of his mouth and contemplated it a moment. "Couple of years after you left I guess. His wife was an Easterner. Thought she could get him to go back East with her. Guess she thought he had some money too. She didn't like it here. Wasn't temperamentally suited to the Cabots. Took off one night and left him and the boy. Never been back since."

Wondering why Angus was being more communicative about Geoffrey than he had been about Lynn, I shifted from one foot to the other and waited patiently.

"Some people say," Angus continued, "that King helped her leave, but . . ."

I knew better than to ask him to go on.

"Bruce and Carole," I finally ventured. "They've had no children?"

"Nope. She's not the motherly type."

I thought for a moment about Carole and agreed with his assessment. Angus got up and started to leave the room, pausing as he walked past me to put his hand on my arm. He scowled at me, but his tone was gentle.

"I don't know what kind of stuff you're made of. I've my doubts. I've been around here a long time. Seen the Cabots come and seen some of 'em go. Something's wrong up there. It's gonna take everything you've got to deal with it.

"And be careful," he warned over his shoulder as he left the room.

———◆———

I was dumbfounded. I had expected anything from Angus but this. It was the third warning I had had today. Angus had increased my suspicions without adding to my knowledge. I couldn't help but be apprehensive about what the evening would hold.

I looked at my watch. It was 3:30. I still had plenty of time before my command performance at the Castle, so I decided to drive to the state highway junction to talk to Sarah Gibson, the local antique dealer, about buying the furniture in the house.

Sarah Gibson was a tall, large woman who had gone flabby in middle age. She looked older than her years. Close to sixty of them, I guessed. Gray hair topped her heavily lined face. Her skin was leathery from years of exposure to the sun. She wore jeans and a man's summer shirt, tucked in loosely so that it billowed out at her waist. I found her in her garden, at the back of the antique shop, energetically pulling weeds. She looked up as I called her name, rocked back on her heels, and wiped the perspiration from her forehead with the back of her hand, leaving a smudge of dirt.

As soon as I mentioned who I was and why I had come to see her, she turned into a calculating machine. Nodding as I described the furniture in the house, she asserted. "Yes, I know the house. Been there, in fact. That desk is a beauty. Been wanting to get my hands on one like that. The rest of the furniture I don't remember so well, but from the sounds of it there's probably not much that would interest me. I mean to say not much that will bring good prices as antiques. 'Course, folks always need second-hand furniture cheap. I'll have to go up and look it over, but I might be able to give you three hundred or so for the whole lot.

I'm really doing you a favor to take some of that stuff off your hands. Might be better off leaving the appliances in the house. Can't do much with old appliances these days except throw them out on the dump." Her voice was strident, and she spoke rapidly as if she didn't have enough time to say everything.

She stopped for a moment and looked at me with sudden recognition. "Oh, yes. You're the one that almost married Bruce Cabot years ago. You've gotten better looking. Too bad he didn't marry you. That wife of his . . ." She shook her head. Sarah Gibson, I was discovering, was a gossip. "She's a real— what do you call them—a nemfomaniac. Can't keep her eyes off men. A real disgrace, it is. Why, the way she's been carrying on with Geoff Cabot all these years is terrible. And him with that little boy. They allus said his wife didn't like it here, but I figured —and I'm not the only one mind you—that she left because of that woman."

I hated gossip, especially small-town gossip. Most of the time it was meant to be harmless, but somehow it never was. All too often it was poisonous, petty, malicious. I disliked myself for listening to Sarah's chatter, but I was ready to grasp at any kind of information I could get.

"It's just like the Cabots to carry on among themselves," Sarah was saying. "With blood like that." She shook her head. I wondered what she meant.

"I was real sorry when your father went. Now, he was a good man—John Trent. I allus thought it was a bit queer, him just disappearing like that. My husband, Ezra, he was alive then. He went on the search parties, but they never found anything. Not even when they brought the dogs in. Ezra allus used to say it was queer. Used to say that John Trent wasn't a man who'd get lost in the mountains, and everybody knew that he didn't like to hunt, so he couldn't have shot himself or anything like that. But King Cabot said he must have had some kind of accident, and if King Cabot says it . . ." She broke off and looked at me, as if to chide me for taking so long to come back.

"Them Cabots," she muttered fiercely. "They're high and mighty up there."

It was then that I remembered who she was. Her name had been Sarah Hazzard when I was growing up, and she had worked for the Cabots until Elizabeth had fired her suddenly for no apparent reason. A few years after that the woman had left Kingsville, but sometime during my absence she must have come back with a husband.

I was unsettled by her intimations that there was something strange about my father's death. Was it merely idle gossip or did Sarah know something? I decided to try to draw her out.

"Do you really think my father could have met with—foul play?"

Her mouth snapped shut like a turtle's beak. "I ain't saying that. I just said it was queer, that's all." She wouldn't elaborate.

I gave her the key to the house, asked her to look at the furniture and give me a price. Then, deeply disturbed by her comments, I left.

◆

I walked into the bar at the hotel and told Angus to give me a bottle of gin, a bottle of vermouth and some ice. He looked at me for a long time, then went behind the bar and handed me the two bottles and a tumbler of ice. He didn't say anything but watched me as I took them, walked out of the bar and up the stairs to my room. I kicked off my shoes, flexed my toes in relief, sat down on the somewhat rumpled bed and mixed myself a very dry martini.

I drank and smoked and stared at the wall trying to sort out what I knew. My father had somehow come into possession of land on Cottonwood Creek. There were no papers on the land except a deed in his name and a title that hadn't been kept up for nearly seventy-five years. That in itself was strange. "Queer" as Sarah Gibson would have said. Then, after giving Paul Darcey his power of attorney he had disappeared without a trace. Earlier I had wondered if he had planned his disappearance. Now I was faced with the possibility that he was indeed dead, and that it hadn't been an accident. But who? And why? Did it have anything to do with the property? Had he, perhaps, suspected something would happen to him? I was faced with a burgeoning series of questions and no answers.

I fixed another martini and switched my thoughts to my upcoming encounter with the Cabots. A host of butterflies began swarming in my stomach. It was not going to be an easy evening. I remembered Sarah's comment that Carole had been playing around with Geoff. I wondered if there was any truth in it. From what I remembered of Geoff—I stopped my conjecture. Lynn had certainly changed; perhaps he had too.

I drained the last of the martini and dressed quickly. I had never been one to primp. When I finished I looked in the rather wavy mirror above the much-painted bureau. Not bad, I said to myself, glad that I had thought to pack a few dresses along with my jeans. I might be plain, but I had learned to accentuate my green eyes and to wear high-necked dresses with rolled collars, which set off my shag hair cut. Grinning at my reflection, suddenly I thought that even the Cabots might be a bit surprised.

———◆———

The road to the Castle went past the Colvada mill, snaked along the side of the canyon and then up six torturous switchbacks. I parked in the circular driveway, got out of the car and paused, listening for the sound of Rob Roy Falls. The waterfall ended in a huge pool perhaps five hundred yards to my right. I could see the gleam of the water through the trees. I caught the hushed roar and smiled to myself. I took two deep breaths to still the butterflies and went up the steps to ring the bell.

Lynn answered the door. Rich as they were, the Cabots used few servants. Sometimes there had been a live-in cook, but more often they simply had a maid who came up from town several times during the week. Other than that, they lived apart from the town they owned.

Lynn's eyes swept over me. I could tell that she was a little surprised and perhaps even a bit pleased. I couldn't blame her after the way I'd looked this afternoon.

"Jenny. You're prompt. Elizabeth will like that. Come in." Her voice seemed to come from a distance. Again I was impressed by her lack of genuine cordiality. As she led the way down the hall, I could see that her face was still guarded and serious—her eyes still somber. "King wanted to talk to you before dinner. He's in the library. I think you know the way." Perfunctorily, she pointed up the hall.

She left me and I walked to the end of the hall, opened the heavy oak doors and stepped into the library. It was a large room, taking up the entire cliff side of the house. The walls were paneled with oak and lined from floor to ceiling with books. A fire was burning in the fireplace against the right wall. There was a rich oriental carpet on the floor, several deep comfortable chairs were scattered around and a huge walnut desk took up most of the left-side of the room.

Kingston Cabot was lounging in one of the chairs facing the fireplace. He stood up as he heard the door click shut. He was a tall, lean, sinewy man with blond hair that was streaked with silver. He wore a tan cotton turtleneck, a soft brown cashmere V-neck sweater and a sport coat that matched his dark green slacks. He had an easy, commanding air about him. He had aged in ten years. He looked a bit weathered—like a rugged, outdoor ad—but he didn't look his fifty-five years. I could see his piercing blue eyes across the room. That deep, ice-blue was a Cabot trait, but of the children only Geoffrey had inherited them. Both Bruce and Lynn had their mother's brown eyes.

"Jenifer." He smiled at me, strode easily across the room, took my hand and led me toward a chair. "Come. Sit down. The rest of the family will be down shortly, but I wanted to talk to you for a moment." Here was the warmth and friendliness I'd missed in Lynn.

He picked up a cigarette from an ash tray and inhaled deeply. "I suppose we're all surprised that you've come back after such a long time. I won't ask your reasons. They're your own. You always were a quiet, sensitive girl as I remember, and I'm sure that whole thing with Bruce was painful." The corner of his mouth lifted in a slight grimace, but his ice-blue eyes, for all their surface warmth, were measuring me very carefully.

King leaned forward in his chair, waving his hand slightly.

"But that's not what I wanted to say to you. Your father was one of my most loyal and trusted employees. He took a great deal of the burden of running the mines from me. He was more than an employee. He was a good friend. I deeply regret the indefiniteness about his death. I want you to know that we tried very hard to find him, but . . ." He shook his head. "You know these mountains. They're cruel and treacherous and massive."

I looked at him steadily, trying to balance his statement with Sarah Gibson's gossipy hints. There was no question but that King's statements should be more reliable. Still, I couldn't rid myself of all my doubts.

He smiled, his eyes crinkling at the corners and suddenly coming alive. "I didn't really mean to make a speech. All this is only to say that as John Trent's daughter I welcome you back to Kingsville, and if there's anything—anything at all—that I can do to help you, please don't hesitate to come to me."

I smiled back at him. I was wondering if perhaps I had just received another warning. As John Trent's daughter I was welcome, but as Jenifer Trent, a woman who had once loved his son . . .

"Thank you," I told him. "That's very kind. I'll only be here long enough to take care of the estate."

We both stood up as the door opened and Elizabeth Cabot swept in. King pulled my hand through his arm. "Elizabeth," he bantered fondly, "I suppose you've come to scold me for keeping our guest to myself."

She was a handsome large-boned woman, with long auburn hair and wide-set brown eyes. She was slightly taller than I, and she carried herself with a grace large women seldom achieve. She seemed to flow into the room. She was dressed in a floor-length yellow flowered dress which emphasized her size. Her summer tan had brought out the freckles on her wide square face. She still looked young, I saw. Beside her, King looked much older and distinguished, while in reality he was only two years older than she.

Elizabeth grasped my free hand, squeezed it, and leaned over to kiss my cheek. "Jenifer, my dear. How very nice to have you back. It's been much too long. And Kingston has been monopolizing you. Everyone is in the dining room, and I think if we wait much longer things will get cold."

I murmured hello, basking in the glow created by her vibrant welcome. Elizabeth had that effect I remembered. She took charge of a situation without seeming to dominate it. She was a supremely confident woman.

Elizabeth took King's other arm, and we went down the hall to the dining room. She kept up a running commentary for the short distance, apparently wanting to put me at ease.

It was a large, well-proportioned room, dominated by the round walnut table and the high-backed caned chairs. A chandelier hung over the table, which was set with the Cabot silver made, I remembered, from the silver taken by the first Kingston Cabot from the King and Queen Mine—the richest strike ever made by the Cabot-owned Colvada Mining Company. Several buffets and a china closet lined the walls of the room. At the far end was a door leading into the kitchen.

The Cabots were all there. Lynn and Paul Darcey were talking quietly, young Christopher was staring out the window looking toward Mithral Falls. Carole, who looked even more stunning than I'd remembered, was hanging onto Bruce in an apparent attempt to demonstrate marital conviviality. An arm resting on the mantle, Geoffrey Cabot was staring into the ashes of the fireplace. Elizabeth continued talking as we entered the room.

"I managed to wrest Jenifer away from Kingston. Jenifer, you remember everyone I think except for Paul and Christopher. Paul." Her tone was a command. Paul Darcey looked up from his conversation with Lynn and walked across the room.

"Miss Trent," he greeted me. "Welcome to the Castle." Seeing Elizabeth's sharp look, he added, "We met this morning. I *am* her father's lawyer, Elizabeth."

"Of course, Paul. How silly of me to forget. Paul spends a good deal of his time with us," she explained to me. "Or perhaps I should say with Lynn." There was a curious undertone to her comment that I couldn't define.

"And Christopher," she continued. "Come here, Chris."

The boy walked slowly toward us, looking steadily at his grandmother. "This is Geoffrey's son, Christopher."

"Hello, Miss Trent." He held out his hand and I shook it. He regarded me gravely, waiting I suppose for me to say something about meeting him. I smiled at him reassuringly.

Bruce cut into the dramatics of the scene his mother had set up.

"Jenny." He broke out of Carole's grasp and came over to me. He hadn't changed much; he was a little heavier, his blond hair, a little longer in the modern style, had grown down over his ears. He stood easily, almost cockily, a slight grin on his face. He put his hands on my shoulders and kissed me lightly on the cheek. Then he stood back to look at me. "It's wonderful to see you again. You look great."

My heart thudded heavily, but whether it was from the butterflies for old time's sake, or because I was still in love with Bruce Cabot, I couldn't determine. With an effort, I forced myself to gaze at him steadily and I felt as if I could hear the shallow, bated breathing of everyone in the room.

"Hello, Bruce," I said evenly.

We stared at each other for a moment longer, and then Carole assertively recaptured Bruce's arm. "Yes, Jenny. It's been such a long time . . ." She let the sentence hang suggestively. She leaned against Bruce, her body exuding a lazy, confident sexuality. I appraised her carefully. Carole had a small face that could have been chiseled from Carrara marble. Each feature was in perfect proportion from her narrow green eyes and her short straight nose, to her sharp chin and perfectly bowed lips. Her long, straight blond hair fell around her face and down her back. She was a bit shorter than I, small-boned with a stunning figure.

I stared at her. "Yes. Hasn't it." I countered her coolly.

Elizabeth took control again, smoothly. "You remember Geoffrey of course. Geoffrey, you're being very antisocial." As always, when she spoke to her eldest son, Elizabeth's tone sharpened a little. It was no secret that she didn't like him.

I remembered hearing the story from childhood. Elizabeth

had married Philip Cabot, King's younger brother. Geoffrey was their son. When Philip had been killed in a mining accident, Elizabeth had married King. When the twins were born, Elizabeth doted on them, especially Bruce. She had never made any effort to be anything other than civil to her first son. I had always wondered why.

Geoffrey straightened as his mother chided him and threw his cigarette into the ashes. He was taller and leaner than Bruce. He had a long face, tight, narrow lips, a straight, thin nose, and curly black hair that fell onto a high forehead. His deep-set blue eyes were masked and he wore a dour, melancholy expression. In a way, he was more a Cabot than either of the twins. Lynn had the Cabot manner, but she had her mother's auburn coloring, while Bruce was a mixture of Elizabeth and King. He had a certain style, but it lacked a sinewy hardness that marked King and Geoff.

"Sorry, Elizabeth," Geoff said. His tone was neutral, distant. He nodded his head slightly in recognition. "Jenny."

We were all still on edge, not knowing quite what to expect of each other. King, apparently deciding that Elizabeth's show had run its course, took over. "Elizabeth, where's that dinner that was getting cold?" he asked dryly.

Dinner went smoothly, despite the undercurrents. King and Elizabeth took charge of the conversation, with Lynn, Bruce and Paul contributing. Carole spoke only when she could make an obvious jibe at me. Geoffrey said nothing. He was brooding and taciturn, just as I had remembered him.

It was because of King that the subject came up. He was talking about the developers who had recently moved into every part of the West. "I'm against it," he said vigorously. "I've refused to sell any of our land to them, and I've used my influence with the Forest Service to see that they don't get a permit for a recreational area."

"That explains why they've come to me," I commented. "They want to buy the land Father owned on Cottonwood Creek. I wondered why, of all the places around here, they would choose that. Apparently, it's because King has blocked them from the better sites."

I had spoken blithely, but suddenly I noticed that Elizabeth looked vaguely discomforted. I caught Lynn and Paul exchanging quick glances. King looked at me for a long moment.

"Your father owned land on Cottonwood?" he asked carefully, fingering his fork.

"Yes." So, I thought, I might not be so far-fetched with my suspicions after all. Surely King Cabot would know who owned every foot of the Kingsville Box, and yet he was clearly surprised to hear of my father's property. I couldn't help feeling it was significant.

"You never mentioned it to us, Paul," Elizabeth reproved him gently.

Paul Darcey smiled, but his voice was cool. "I don't discuss clients' affairs. If the clients wish to discuss them," he shrugged, turning his palms upward in a gesture of resignation.

"Well," Lynn jumped into the conversation. "Enough of these gloomy matters. The ski hills are not upon us yet, thank God. We'll just have to work on persuading Jenny not to sell, won't we, King?"

"Indeed."

"Jenny," Lynn continued with a kind of false gaiety. It hurt me to see her trying to be her old self and failing. "Do you remember all the times we used to play at the Rob Roy? It's even more desolate and wonderful now. We'll have to go up there soon. Tomorrow maybe. You still ride, don't you? It's much better than taking the jeep."

I saw rather than heard young Christopher's wary intake of breath. If he had known me better, he would have realized that I wouldn't betray him. "The Rob Roy. Yes, I'd love to see it again. As for riding, a working girl doesn't get much chance, but I'm sure it will come back."

"Along with bruises and sores, darling," Carole put in cuttingly. She was a superb horsewoman, I remembered.

I stared at her across the table. "Of course," I told her coldly. "That's taken for granted."

"You didn't use to."

"Really? Well, perhaps I've changed."

Elizabeth cut into the exchange, "Why, Jenny, you know I never even thought to ask you. I assume you're staying at Angus'."

"Yes. It's a little quaint, but for the time I'll be here it serves my purposes. And he's a dear."

"Nonsense," Elizabeth insisted firmly, suddenly dominating the conversation. "You can't stay in that wretched hotel. After all you're practically one of the family. Your father was very dear to us. You must stay here. Kingston, don't you agree that it's ridiculous for Jenifer to stay with Angus when she could be perfectly comfortable here?"

King smiled fondly at her and heartily reinforced Elizabeth's invitation. "By all means. You're absolutely right, my dear. Jenny, I should have thought of it myself. Of course you must stay with us."

Once again I had a Cabot invitation before me and I must decide what to do about it. I knew that I couldn't hesitate.

"It will be like old times," Bruce put in eagerly. "You, Lynn and me. Do come." He smiled at me, and I began to feel distinctly uncomfortable. My butterflies, which I had almost forgotten, returned.

Carole was clearly furious. She didn't say anything, but her jaw clamped in a hard line and her eyes snapped angrily. Elizabeth looked at her son as if trying to calculate how much of his enthusiasm was real, and then reissued her invitation. "I'm not going to take no for an answer, Jenny. It's unthinkable to have you staying down there. Geoffrey can go down with you tonight and get your bags. Geoffrey?"

For the first time in a long while I noticed Geoffrey Cabot. He was tracing the pattern on the lace tablecloth with the end of a spoon. He looked up briefly. "If you wish, Elizabeth." His tone was tired.

"Geoff doesn't have to go," Bruce said quickly. "I can do it."

It was time to make my wishes felt. "No. That's quite all right.

I'm a bit tired. It's been a long day and I really can't see repacking tonight. Tomorrow will be fine."

I watched Lynn. She seemed a bit surprised that I was so decisive. Elizabeth, having won the main bout, graciously acceded. "Geoffrey will come down in the morning then. Say about ten. That will give you time to sleep in a bit. This is your vacation, isn't it? You can come up and have a late breakfast. Then you and Lynn can go up to the Rob Roy . . ."

I broke in before she finished. I had to make it clear that I was going to be free to make my own schedule. "Please don't bother about breakfast. I can only agree to stay here if you promise not to fuss over me. I have some things to take care of with Paul in the morning. Lynn and I can arrange our expedition later. We do have almost two weeks, and I plan to do a lot of exploring of old territory." I used the manner I had developed for distressed passengers and irate employees—matter-of-fact, almost terse, but managing to be tactful at the same time. I smiled and waited for the reaction.

It was subtle. King nodded his head slightly, and Geoff deigned to look up from the tablecloth to stare at me momentarily before returning to his doodling. Again, Lynn and Paul exchanged glances. Elizabeth's look I couldn't decipher. She wasn't offended, but neither was she pleased. She reacted gracefully, as always.

"Of course, my dear. You must feel free to do as you please."

Despite the cordiality, I was uneasy. I wondered if I was doing a wise thing. I had enough to deal with in trying to find out about my father. Castle Cabot seemed to be a tangled spider's web of cross purposes and thickly veiled emotions and I, like the proverbial fly, was stepping into it.

CHAPTER 3

I slept late the next morning. Consequently, I was just finishing my cup of instant coffee when I heard the knock. Assuming it was Angus, I flung a "come in" over my shoulder and continued to sip my coffee while absently trying to fluff my hair into some sort of shape. I was thinking about ways to find out how my father had gotten his property.

"Sorry to bother you, Jenny. I stopped by before, but Angus said you weren't up yet."

I jumped slightly and then turned to see Geoffrey Cabot standing in the doorway. He was dressed for work this morning —jeans and a light blue summer shirt, open at the collar. The sleeves of the shirt were rolled up above his elbows and he wore leather gloves. He stood easily, his eyes narrowed guardedly, as they always were. I hoped that he hadn't noticed my surprised lurch, but, of course, he had.

"I didn't mean to startle you," he apologized perfunctorily.

"You didn't really. I wasn't expecting you, that's all."

The corner of his mouth lifted in a slight grimace. "You shouldn't tell people to come in when you don't know who you're expecting," he told me grimly. "Elizabeth wanted me to take your bags up to the Castle."

"Oh. Of course. I'd forgotten. I overslept and haven't quite gotten organized yet." I stopped myself from going on with my idiotic explanation. Before this brooding, strong, self-possessed man I was babbling like a moron. Pulling myself together I smiled a bit ruefully at him. "What I'm trying to say is that I've not packed yet. Could you wait a few minutes? It won't take long." That was better.

He didn't reply. Instead, he leaned against the door frame, pulled a cigarette out of his pocket and lit it. He watched me with his hooded eyes as I opened my suitcases and quickly filled them. I felt vaguely uncomfortable. He reminded me of a falcon, hooded and on a chain but ready to strike the moment he was unloosed.

I finished and looked around the room, making sure that I hadn't forgotten anything. "Here you are. Could you tell Elizabeth that I'm not sure what my schedule is going to be today and that I'll give her a call this afternoon."

"Sure." He straightened and came across the room. He stubbed the cigarette out in the ash tray on the bureau, then picked up the two suitcases. Before he turned to leave, he stopped for a moment. He looked at me, his eyes opening slightly. His gaze was piercing as though he were trying to see through me. To find what, I didn't know. I forced myself to return his look, staring into the ice-blue frozenness of his eyes. Outwardly I remained calm, but I felt completely unnerved. Whatever it was between us hovered in the background, unknown and rather ominous.

I broke it. "Thanks for coming by, Geoff. I know you're busy." It was a dismissal, although I hadn't intended for it to be so abrupt. The hooded look returned, sliding back into place like the well-known mask it was. He nodded in acknowledgment of my thanks, moved to the door and left without saying anything more.

I shivered and sat down heavily on the rickety stool by the bureau. Absently, I ran my hand through my hair. I had been stunned by several things since I had returned to Kingsville. By Christopher. By the change in Lynn. But nothing had affected me like Geoffrey Cabot's look. I suddenly realized that he frightened me.

Outwardly, there was nothing about him that should be intimidating. He was basically the same withdrawn, laconic man I had remembered. Still, I couldn't escape the memory of his icy, intent eyes. I shook my head and turned to stare at myself in the wavy mirror.

When I had decided to come to Kingsville I had known I would have to face the Cabots, especially Bruce. I had envisioned it as a test of my maturity and sense of myself. I would see Bruce, realize how foolish I had been, and the scar would melt into the flesh—there but nearly indistinguishable. Now, I began to realize that it was going to be more complicated than that. The strand of my twenty-nine years was entangled with the web which bound the Cabots together. Bruce, Lynn, Geoffrey, even young Christopher—they all touched my life. In accepting Elizabeth's invitation, I had chosen to involve myself with the Cabots once again. One could not be a passive observer at Castle Cabot. There were too many emotional undercurrents for that. I knew that I was efficient, competent, controlled, but I didn't know if I was hard enough, tough enough, strong enough to meet the Cabots on their own ground.

I was at the bottom of the stairs on my way to see Paul Darcey when I met Bruce.

"Jenny," he hailed me, smiling broadly. " 'Morning."

His eyes swept over me in that intimate way he had. It had always affected me, excited me, and that, I told myself with resignation, hadn't changed. I felt as though he were embracing me. Out of the corner of my eye I could see Angus standing in the doorway to the bar watching the little scene. I was uncomfortable, but I wasn't going to make a fool of myself over Bruce Cabot this time. I came down the last two steps, smiled briefly, almost mechanically.

"Hullo, Bruce. This is a surprise."

His grin, if possible, broadened. "Good. I was hoping it would be. I thought I'd run your bags up to the Castle."

"Thanks, but you're a little late. Geoff has already stopped by." I was trying to be cordial but not warm. I didn't know if I was succeeding.

A look of annoyance crossed his face momentarily. It was

gone so quickly I wasn't sure that I hadn't imagined it. His tone, when he spoke, was joking. "Well, well. Old Geoff beat me to the punch again. Don't suppose there's anything I can help you with?" It was a suggestion.

"Afraid not. I'm meeting Paul Darcey, and I'm late as it is."

"I wouldn't worry about that. Paul's got a lot of time. It's pretty quiet up here in the Box. Not too many people need lawyers."

"I guessed that much from seeing his office," I laughed, remembering my impression of Paul Darcey. "But still, I have this thing about punctuality. And I have to settle up with Angus."

He got the hint. "Okay. I'll see you later." It was a promise. He caressed me with his eyes again and then turned and ran, whistling, out of the hotel.

I watched, grateful that he had been persuaded to leave so easily. I wondered if he had meant his looks to be so intimate, or if I had merely wanted to see that almost careless possessiveness? Reality or mirage or desire? I didn't know.

After a moment I walked over to Angus and told him that I would be checking out to go up to the Castle. I paid him for the two nights. He was noncommittal, nodding his head as I spoke. He was getting change for my twenty-dollar bill when he started to speak, almost as though he were talking to himself.

"Been a real interesting morning," he said in his roundabout old-timer's way. "Yep. That it has. Never know how much you can learn just standing in the doorway to the bar. People coming and going."

I broke into his monologue. "Just what are you trying to say, Angus?" I knew he was referring to the fact that both Bruce and Geoffrey had been to the hotel.

He looked at me, his sharp eyes missing neither my outward calm nor my inner irritation. "I don't miss much, lass. You're playing with fire."

I stared at him coldly. "And you're being cryptic again, Angus," I snapped. "Say what you mean."

He wasn't bothered by my abruptness. "I did, Jenifer. I did."

He counted my change out and placed it in my hand. He dropped his put-on chattiness now. "You should know the Cabots well enough by now to know that you'd better be careful. Unless, of course, you didn't learn anything the last time."

I winced. Angus had touched a raw nerve. "You've gotten cruel in your old age, Angus." I whirled and strode out of the hotel.

———◆———

Paul Darcey was waiting at his office. He seemed unconcerned that I was late and asked no questions. He appeared to be a relaxed, easy-going man, but I sensed once again that beneath his lanky, indifferent pose was a keen mind and a steel-trap hardness that I didn't want to arouse. I would have to be careful with him as well.

He suggested that we could see the property better if we rode rather than drove and that the Cabot stables were open to us. I was a little dubious about trying out my rusty horsemanship, but I acceded to his arrangements. We drove to the stables which were along Rob Roy Creek, at the base of the escarpment, and selected a couple of horses. It had been a long time, and Paul good-naturedly helped me saddle and bridle the chestnut mare he had picked out for me.

We rode leisurely back toward Kingsville and then turned up Cottonwood Creek. It was a beautiful, wild alpine canyon that cut back into the San Juans on the south side of the Kingsville Box. The mouth of the canyon was delineated by two steep, thickly wooded hills. The creek rushed among the groves of quaking aspen, cottonwood and stands of pine, picking its way around boulders, tumbling rapidly down the canyon. About five miles upstream, the canyon boxed into shear, grayish-red cliffs, above which towered a group of snow-covered mountains. From the high snowfields, across the velvet-green meadows to the floor of the canyon, water fell in series after series of short, but spectacular waterfalls.

As with most areas in the San Juans, the only access was by a dirt jeep road. Paul and I rode up the dirt track. We didn't talk much at first. I was concentrating on getting back into the swing of riding. I was surprised that it came back so easily, like skiing or riding a bicycle. Soon I felt enough at ease to start feeling Paul Darcey out.

"How did you happen to come to Kingsville?" It was an innocuous question.

He laughed. "I was on my way to LA. Believe it or not I took a wrong turn at the junction, and once I'd seen the Box I knew I couldn't leave."

"I wouldn't imagine there's a lot of work. Kingsville is a dying town."

"I manage. I handle all the Colvada business. I'm not an ambitious man. The Box is a beautiful place. There's a lot of food for the spirit here, even if business isn't overworking me. I enjoy it."

I glanced at him. "Would I be too far off the mark if I guessed that you don't want me to sell to the developers?"

"As your lawyer I can only advise you that it's a monetarily wise thing to do. The property isn't worth much as it is. You can't ranch on it—not the kind of terrain that's back up here in this canyon. And there are no metals in the canyon. Since you'll be going back to the city, there's no real reason for you to keep the land. I assume the money won't be bothersome. It seldom is."

"That's a fine speech from my lawyer. How do you really feel about it?"

"I promise to give generously of my legal opinion. You're paying for it. My private opinion can hardly be of interest to you."

"You underestimate yourself. I'm very interested."

"After you decide what you're going to do I'll tell you what I think about it. How's that?" He had adroitly side-stepped my challenge.

My jaw tightened. Somewhere I had a stubborn streak, and I was beginning to get more than a little irritated by the cat-and-mouse tactics everyone engaged in. Just once I'd like to get a straight answer. With an effort, I covered my annoyance.

"How long ago was it that you made that wrong turn?"

He glanced at me quickly, perhaps to see how I had meant the question. I kept my face emotionless and gazed blandly ahead.

"About five years ago, I guess. It's gone fast."

We were silent for a while. When we were about halfway up the canyon, Paul cut his horse sharply to the left, leaving the road and splashing across the creek. He halted then and began pointing out the boundaries of my property.

"The property lines are a bit vague," he concluded. "It's never been surveyed. If you're seriously considering selling, we'll have to get someone up here to survey it. Why on earth did your father want land up here anyway?" he asked suddenly. As I had the day before, I felt that he was trying to catch me off guard. "Whoever sold it to him must have been relieved."

I wasn't about to answer his question. Wasn't and couldn't. "My father and I weren't close. I have no more knowledge of his motivation than I do of yours." I had tried to be light, but it had come out in a rather chilly tone.

He laughed easily. "Okay. Okay. I've had my hands slapped."

I unbent a little and laughed with him. "Sorry," I apologized. "I didn't mean it that way. I guess I'm a little sensitive about my father."

He immediately became sympathetic. "Parents can be difficult, and they say that the formative years—you know all that psychotherapeutic stuff. I sometimes wonder about Christopher—" His voice trailed off and he left the thought uncompleted.

I decided to pick up on the topic he had unwittingly opened. "Yes. I think I know what you mean. He seemed such a quiet, sad boy. But then Geoff was somewhat the same way. His father's death and Elizabeth's remarriage to King must have hit him hard. And now Christopher with no mother and a withdrawn father—" This time I broke off. It hit too close to home.

Paul perceived the obvious but unspoken comparison. "Lynn and I are quite fond of the boy, but he's hard to get close to. As you say, he's like his father, and Geoffrey is impossible to approach. I've often thought of talking to him about Chris, but . . . I don't know. It's not really my place."

"Why doesn't Lynn talk to him if she feels so strongly about it? She was closer to Geoff than any of us, and she was never one to let much stop her."

"Lynn's gotten cautious in her old age." I wondered if I was imagining the tinge of pain in his voice. "Besides," he added, "Geoff is even more insular since his marriage broke up. Or at least that's what Lynn and King say."

"What happened to the marriage anyway?" I knew Angus' explanation, and Sarah Gibson's, but I thought that Paul, as a virtual member of the family, might have a different viewpoint.

He became reticent suddenly, as if regretting that he had opened up with me for a moment. "She was an Eastern girl who didn't like living here. I guess she also thought Geoff had money. Or at least that's what everyone says. I wasn't here then."

It was Angus' version without the innuendos. I had the feeling that Paul Darcey knew more about the Cabots than he let on. I wondered how close he was to Kingston.

He straightened in his saddle and his tone became more businesslike. "Now, if we ride up around the bend, you'll see where the developers want to build their resort." He kicked his sorrel in motion and I followed suit.

When we finished our tour of inspection and were headed back to the stables I decided to draw him out about Lynn. For a man who was engaged to her, he hadn't talked much about her.

"Angus tells me that you and Lynn are engaged."

"Yes. I've heard those rumors too." His voice was curiously blank.

"Oh, come now, Paul. I can call you Paul, can't I?" I turned on all my charm.

"Let's put it this way. Lynn and I see a lot of each other. One of these days we might get married."

"One of these days?" I asked lightly.

"That's what I said." His tone was irritable. Apparently there was more trouble here than I had thought.

He saw my startled look and tried to apologize. "Look, I'm sorry, Miss Trent. Jenifer. I know you're an old friend of Lynn's, but I'd rather not discuss it."

I had always been poignantly aware of my own pain, trying, sometimes without success, to shut it out when it became unbearable. But my return to Kingsville was forcing me to become aware of the pain of others. So far, few had been immune. Elizabeth and King perhaps. But the rest of the Cabots—there was more pain there than I wanted to deal with, more than I felt capable of dealing with.

"I didn't mean to pry," I said gently. "I guess what I was really getting at is that Lynn has changed, and I was wondering why."

"You remember her from a long time ago, and memories get warped. She's the same Lynn I've always known." It was a straight enough answer, but I sensed that he knew what I meant and he didn't like it either.

I dropped the topic and went back to small talk. Soon, we cantered into the stables, rubbed the horses down and then set off for the bank. It was time to tackle the mysterious box.

———◆———

Paul parked my car in front of the bank, alongside the high, broken cement sidewalk. Gold lettering on the plate-glass windows proclaimed that the Kingsville Trust Company had been founded in 1846. It was somehow abrasive to see the modern low brick building nestled among the old two-story, wood-frame store fronts that lined the main street of Kingsville. Many of them were abandoned and boarded up, relics of the town's onetime prominence among Colorado mining camps. Their foundations had settled, and they leaned precariously, threatening to collapse at any moment. Looking at them, one would hardly guess that a family as wealthy as the Cabots made their home in Kingsville.

We entered the bank and Paul introduced me to Peter Holt, the bank manager. We exchanged pleasantries, and then he led us to a small room at the rear of the bank. Against the wall were several rows of safety deposit boxes. He and Paul produced their keys, and he unlocked the panel, pulling out a long brown metal lockbox. Peter Holt handed me the box and offered me the use of his office.

I cradled the box under my arm, walked into his office and closed the door. I selected the smaller key that I had found in the desk and fit it into the lock, holding my breath as I turned it. The lock hadn't been used in years. The key grated reluctantly but turned. There was a slight click and the top popped up. My fingers trembled a bit as I opened it. Inside were several pieces of paper, a sample sack, a wedding band and some old silver dollars.

I went through the papers first. I quickly glanced over my father and mother's marriage certificate, an old insurance policy, the deed to the house, the certificates of Cabot stock. There was an envelope addressed to my father. The back address read Alex Grainger, 10 Lead Street, Cortez, Colorado. I tried to make out the postmark, but it was too faint. There was nothing inside the envelope.

I leafed through some uninteresting papers until I came to an official-looking document bearing the seal of Colorado. I turned to the second page and discovered that here, at least, was part of the answer I had been looking for. It was the original deed to the Cottonwood property. I glanced over the boundary definitions and saw that they were basically the same as those Paul Darcey had pointed out to me. The most interesting part of the deed was the name of the owner—Philip Anthony Cabot.

I put the paper down and walked away from the desk. This was a turn of the screw I hadn't expected, even in my wildest imaginings. Philip Cabot had owned the land and had given or sold it to my father. But why? Father hadn't been close to Philip. It was Kingston he admired. There would have been no reason for Philip to have given him the land, yet there was no bill of sale. No transferal of title. Either he, or he and Philip Cabot, had made sure that there would be no record of their transaction. Again, the nagging question returned. Why?

King must suspect that the land had belonged to his dead brother, I thought. That would account for his surprise at my announcement that the developers wanted to buy my land. And Elizabeth? She had been married to Philip. Did she also know that the land should be the Cabots'? Perhaps it should even be hers. I had no idea what the terms of Philip's will were. At least this solved the mystery of why everything would revert to Geoffrey if I were to die. That provision in my father's will coupled with this new discovery convinced me that there was something illegal about the ownership of the land.

Sternly reminding myself that I would get nowhere asking rhetorical questions, I turned back to my examination of the box. I opened the sample sack and upended it. Like the envelope, it was empty. Absently, I put my hand inside, wearing the sack like a mitten. My fingers touched paper. Puzzled I pulled it out. Scrawled on the torn scrap of paper were several cryptic words, separated by dashes. It had been written in haste, but I recognized my father's handwriting.

MITHRAL STAIR—FLYING DUTCHMAN—HANGING WALL—
GRUBSTAKE—FIFTH LEVEL

I scratched my head in bewilderment. I could make no sense of it. Hanging wall was a geologic term, although I wasn't exactly certain about its meaning. Flying Dutchman and Grubstake sounded like the names of mines, but where they were I had no idea. Mithral Stair must be related in some way to Mithral Basin or the falls, but again I came up against a dead end.

I sensed that the paper and its elusive message were important. I replaced everything but the envelope and the scrap of paper. The lockbox which had lain unopened for so many years had yielded a strange treasure. My glance caught the keys lying on the desk. One down, one to go I thought. Finding the lock for the other key wouldn't be as easy.

———◆———

As we left the bank, I could sense Paul's curiosity about what had been in the box. Wanting to divert him, I asked him to take care of finding a realtor who would handle selling the house. He wanted me to meet with Greenberg, the man representing the ski developers, but I stalled him, saying that I wanted a chance to look at the property again and to think about what I wanted to do with it. I had an idea that Alex Grainger might be able to tell me something helpful. The name wasn't familiar, but he must have had some importance for my father to have kept his address. The contents of the box definitely seemed to be restricted to things Father had considered significant.

Telling Paul I was going to see Sarah Gibson again about the furniture, I left him in Kingsville and drove slowly down the Box toward the junction. As I drove I thought about Paul. Being with him today had added another dimension to the picture I had of him. Instinctively, I liked and trusted him, yet I had some nagging doubts about what his interests were. He was closely connected with the Cabots and must have access to all their papers. I wondered if he realized the land had once belonged to Philip.

The drive to Cortez was a pleasant one. The highway cut south paralleling the mountains. High bridges spanned the narrow river valleys that cut down from the San Juans. Occasionally the road rose and wound over long, hogbacked ridges. After an hour I swept up over the last hogback and started dropping down onto the outer edge of the high Colorado Plateau. The land flattened, becoming dotted with mesquite and purple sage. The rocks were no longer warped in convoluted agony, but ran straight and true, layer upon layer of varying thicknesses and multitudinous colors, carved into strange and terrifying beauty.

Cortez was a typical Southwestern town. I drove past the Catholic church and stopped at a phone booth where I looked Alex Grainger up in the phone book. I almost doubted that I could find him so I nearly overlooked the small entry sandwiched between other names. I checked the address; it was the same as the one on the envelope. I decided not to call. In ten more minutes, after asking directions at a gas station, I pulled up in front of a small, whitewashed, adobe house, set back from the street. There was a pockmarked lawn that looked like a miniature battleground and a ragged, broken cement walk that led up to the house. The screen door hung crookedly on its hinges and protested with low squeaks as I pulled it open. Clearly, Alex Grainger was not well off.

He came to the door and I introduced myself. He was in his

early fifties, short, thin and stoop-shouldered with curly sandy hair, graying at the temples, and enormous round brown eyes. He led the way to a small living room near the back of the house. The carpet was threadbare and the arms of the chairs were covered with lace doilies, hiding worn spots, I suspected.

"I won't take up much of your time," I began, plunging into the reason for my visit. "I've just returned to Kingsville and have been going through my father's things. I found your name and address in a lockbox, and it occurred to me that there must have been some reason for my father to have put it there. I was hoping you could tell me how you knew him."

He fingered a doily. "I used to be an assayer. John came to me because he was obsessed with the idea that there was a strike to be made on Cottonwood Creek. I tried to persuade him that it was futile to look there, but he was totally irrational about the subject. I helped him map the area, looking for formations that might be promising, and analyzed the samples he brought me over the years. He did manage to find a small deposit of nickel, but it wasn't large enough to do anything with and it was an isolated pocket."

"How long ago was this?"

"Oh, heavens. He came to me first about fifteen, maybe even twenty years ago. He kept coming until just before he died. I must admit I was worried about him the last time I saw him. I always wondered if perhaps he didn't take his own life."

I tried to hide my shock. Sarah Gibson had implied murder. Here was another possibility. "Why do you say that?"

"He was very disturbed—almost, well crazy sounding at times. He told me he was going to give it all up, that there wasn't anything on the creek. Said it didn't matter any more. He felt that he'd wasted his life chasing rainbows. I've seen it often enough. Men get obsessed by metals and the money they bring. By silver and gold and all the rest. It destroys them eventually. That's what happened to your father I'm afraid. When he finally admitted defeat he couldn't go on. There are all kinds of treasure and the least of them are gold and silver, but John never knew that."

I cut into his philosophizing. "Can you remember anything specific that he said?"

He frowned in recollection. "No," he said slowly. "No, I'm sorry. I can't."

I talked to him for a while longer, querying him about the property, but he had no further information and finally I thanked him for his time and left. I had now learned why and from whom my father had acquired the Cottonwood property, but not how.

<hr>

It was after four when I got back to Kingsville. The Cabots didn't dine until seven, and since I didn't want to have to spend too much time at the Castle before dinner I decided to drive up Cottonwood and look at the property again. I needed some time to think about my father. I drove carefully up the narrow dirt road. At a turnout near the boundaries of the property, I parked the car and walked over to the stream. My eyes swept over the speckled gneiss formations along the canyon walls and stopped on the overgrown remains of an old tunnel. With sudden decision I waded across the stream and through the brush, the branches of sage slapping at my legs.

A cave-in had blocked all but the top foot of the tunnel. Clumps of grass and brush were growing in the rocks. Broken timbers hung, truncated at the roof of the adit. No one had disturbed the area for a long time. I turned and walked up the canyon, staying close to the cliff. A few minutes' walk brought me to a large talus pile. Clambering onto it, I chose a large, flat rock bathed in sun, and sat down. A chipmunk came out of his nearby hole, chattered at me and then ducked out of sight. I stretched and closed my eyes against the sun, letting my mind drift.

I thought about my father. I didn't remember much about him when I was young. I had faded but happy snapshots in my memory of myself with my father and mother. Then, suddenly, my mother was no longer there. I had lost my father then. The memory of all the years I had spent alone flooded over me.

I heard him clearing his throat and I recognized his somber, childish tones immediately. "Is something the matter, Miss Trent?"

I opened my eyes and realized that I'd been crying. I felt a perfect fool as I wiped my face with the back of my hand.

"Hullo, Christopher." He was standing about fifteen feet from me, staring at me with his solemn blue eyes.

"I shouldn't have bothered you, but you looked so sad," he said by way of explanation. He was being quite the little gentleman.

I smiled gently at him. "That's all right. I was just remembering things from my childhood. Memories make you sad sometimes. What are you doing all the way up here?"

He shrugged. "Just walking."

"You spend a lot of time by yourself, don't you?"

He didn't answer, even evasively. I decided to try to draw him out, to get him to trust me.

"I never used to come up here much," I told him conversationally. "When Lynn and Bruce and I were growing up our favorite place was the Rob Roy." I chatted on, recounting pieces of my childhood. He sat beside me after a moment and, chewing on a long piece of grass, listened politely. Gradually, in answer to my questions, he told me how he spent his days, about the stray dog he had befriended and how he wished he could have one. He spoke fondly of Lynn, a bit fearfully I thought of Elizabeth and King, and not at all of his father. I felt him relax a little. I was terribly pleased. For some strange reason, this small, vulnerable, lonely boy had begun to matter a great deal to me.

Finally we fell silent. Christopher sat quietly, his father's impenetrable mantle of reserve wrapped around him. I was wondering what to say to him next, so I didn't notice anything until Christopher jumped up, tugging at my arm.

"Come on. Please. Hurry!"

His voice broke, shrill and frightened on the last word. He glanced quickly up the talus and began bounding down the slope.

My reactions were sluggish. I looked, as he had, up at the cliff and then sat frozen for a moment, an awful wave of fear running through me. A large boulder had come loose from the cliff and was bounding down the talus, its weight and momentum loosening other rocks so that the whole upper third of the rock slide was in grinding motion. It wouldn't be enough to get out of the way of the boulder which was headed directly for me. I had to get off the slide immediately. I could hear the rocks crushing against one another as they moved.

With a surge, the adrenalin began flowing and I followed Christopher's example, leaping up and running heedlessly down the treacherous rock slope. I could feel the sharpness of the rocks through the rubber soles of my tennis shoes, and I had to catch myself several times from falling as my ankles twisted on the loose rocks. My life hung on reaching a grove of cottonwood trees that stood to one side of the talus.

It seemed like an eternity. I couldn't remember having been so frightened before. Dealing with a crisis in San Francisco that involved people was one thing. There were actions you might take to change things. But here, a small natural happening played out to its inexorable end, and the only thing one could do was get out of the way. I leapt off the last few feet of the tumbled mass of rocks like a broad jumper and dashed to the safety of the trees. Christopher was there, looking not at the talus but at the top of the cliff. I followed his gaze for a moment and then turned to watch the huge boulder as it crashed across the creek, tore through some brush and cracked against a medium-sized fir tree, which snapped off and fell with a heavy swishing thud across the creek.

My breath was still coming in fast gasps, both from the exertion and from the close call we had just had. I could see that Christopher was badly frightened, and I resolved that he shouldn't see my own fear. I struggled to control myself, leaning against a tree because my legs were trembling.

"It's a good thing for us that you happened to look up when you did," I told him.

He turned to look at me then. His eyes were huge, like a

Keene painting, and he was shaking. "I'm sorry to leave you up there, but . . ." His voice trailed off.

"Oh, Chris," I murmured. Impulsively, I went over to him and caught him in my arms. He buried his head in my chest, his arms went around my waist and he began sobbing convulsively. I held him, running my hand over his head and talking to him, trying to calm him. The concentration required to reassure him served to quiet my own raw nerves. He needed me just then, not as an individual perhaps, but as someone to cling to. I was determined not to let him down.

At length, he became quiet, but he remained huddled in my arms. I fell silent, thinking it best to let him collect himself. Eventually, he pulled away from me and, regretfully, I let him go. His eyes were red and swollen and I noticed with alarm that his introverted, somber countenance was more pronounced than it had been before.

"I'm sorry, Miss Trent," he said stiffly.

I groaned inwardly. Just when he had been coming out of that terrible, lonely shell a little. "Nonsense," I told him gently. "We're friends, aren't we? You don't have to apologize to friends. And please call me Jenny."

He didn't reply but stood, head down, gazing at the ground. I was puzzled. We had both been scared. Granted, he was a small boy, but there was something strange about his reaction. At first it had been natural. Then suddenly he had pulled himself together and retreated farther away than ever. Unless I was imagining things, he was still very frightened. It wasn't just aftershock I saw in his tense bearing. There was active alarm. I knelt down so that I could look at him. His eyes, hooded now like his father's, were darting from side to side, as though he were waiting for something else to happen.

I thought quickly. He had heard the boulder coming so soon that he had been in no danger from it and certainly had been well off the talus before the movement of the other rocks had reached the level at which we'd been sitting. It was I who had really been in danger because of my slow reaction. Then, too, he'd been looking at the top of the cliff when I'd finally reached him, not at the boulder, not at me.

I stood up, turned and stepped out of the trees a bit, gazing back up at the cliff. I estimated it to be about two hundred feet high. I couldn't remember clearly what the cliff had looked like before, but after a few moments of intensive study I was certain that the rock had not been dislodged from the broken face. Besides, I told myself, the boulder had been round and weathered. Any large hunk of rock that broke loose from the cliff would have been rough, jagged.

I remembered the mysterious rider I had seen at the top of Rob Roy Falls and the shot I had heard. I remembered, too, Angus' cryptic warnings. I narrowed my eyes suddenly, detecting what seemed to be movement in the trees at the top of the cliff. A nasty suspicion began to form in the back of my mind.

I turned back and held out my hand to Christopher. "I've never seen a rock slide right after it happened. Let's go look at the cliff and see where it came from."

He put his hands in his pockets hunching his shoulders. He shook his head once, violently.

"Okay, then. I think I'm going to." I tried to be light and nonchalant about it.

He looked worried. "We should go back to the Castle. It will be time for dinner soon."

"Sure. I'm just going to run up to the top of the cliff, and then we'll go back. If you're anxious to get home, go on ahead. I'll miss your company but . . ."

"Don't go up there." I could hear the fear in his voice. "Please don't."

"Why not, Chris?" I asked softly.

"It's not a good idea," he said. He was casting around for a good excuse, and his hesitation and unsureness were evident in his manner. "It's not safe," he explained hastily, the words tumbling out in a rush. "Those rocks can come down at any minute. We never should have been on the talus. Grandpa King's always warned me. You have to stay away from cliffs like this. You mustn't go up there."

I walked over to him and took hold of his arm lightly. "Look, Christopher, I like you. I want to be your friend. I want to help you. Trust me."

He shook his head. "There's nothing you can do," he said in a small, tight voice.

I wasn't about to give up. Instinctively, I knew that it meant too much to both of us. "It wasn't an accident, was it? That rock couldn't have come from the cliff. Someone pushed it over the edge."

He carefully avoided looking at me. "It's not the first time someone has tried to scare you, is it? That day at the falls. Someone shot at you."

"Please, just leave it alone." He was clearly miserable, alone and frightened.

"I can't do that, Christopher. I'm going up on the cliff. Do you want to come with me?"

I didn't wait for his answer; I knew there wouldn't be one. I began walking down the creek to a point where I could climb back to the top of the cliff. He followed me.

Once on the cliff, I quickly found what I was looking for. The rocks at one spot directly above where we had been sitting were deeply scratched as though a prying instrument of some kind had been used to dislodge the boulder. In the ground was the indentation where the boulder had rested. I walked back in the trees and found horse tracks leading off in the direction of Kingsville. Christopher didn't say anything, merely trudged along beside me. I had told him that someone was trying to scare him, but I knew that I was probably being too lenient. Someone was trying to harm him. But why? Who would want to hurt a nine-year-old boy?

CHAPTER 4

Christopher rode back to Kingsville with me. Acting on a hunch I detoured by the stables. Most of the horses were in their stalls. Only two were missing and after a little prodding Christopher told me they were Carole's and Lynn's.

"Damn," I muttered softly to myself. Neither of them would be strong enough to pry a boulder that size loose. And what motive could they possibly have? Everything was going too fast, getting too serious and I knew so little. I had been so sure that the tracks I had seen atop the cliff were made by one of the Cabot horses. Idly, I patted the horse near me.

I was so preoccupied that it took several moments for me to realize that the big sorrel had been ridden recently—and ridden hard. His flank was wet with perspiration and, as I looked more closely at him, I could see the damp, matted look of his mane and coat. Someone had thrown the saddle and bridle off hastily and left the stables without rubbing him down or currying him. It had been a sorrel, I reminded myself grimly, that I had seen at the top of the falls.

Christopher was watching me, apprehensively, as I examined the horse.

"Whose horse is this, Christopher?"

Typically, he didn't answer. His mouth tightened and he had the small, frightened look of a rabbit when it's cornered. He stood for a moment and then started to run out of the stables, but I anticipated his move and caught him.

"It's important, Christopher. Whose is he? I'll find out eventually anyway. You may as well tell me."

His face twisted and he looked as though he might cry again. He broke away from my grasp and ran out of the stables.

Angrily, I kicked at a nearby bale of hay. I had pushed him too far.

I got back to the Castle after six. I parked the car and was hurrying toward the house, knowing I had little time to shower and change before dinner, when a hand shot out of the bushes grabbing my arm. I jumped and managed to half-stifle a cry of alarm before I recognized Bruce.

"It's only me," he laughed, drawing me toward him. "I want to talk to you before you get monopolized by Mother and King."

I relaxed a bit. "What did you want to talk about?" I managed to say evenly.

He loosened his grip but kept his hand on my arm. "Let's go down toward the falls. We've less chance of having someone barge in on us down there."

I glanced at my watch and then followed him. The roar of Rob Roy Falls became louder. About halfway between the house and the bottom of the falls he stopped, leaned back against a pine and pulled me around to face him. My heart thudded uncertainly, and I tried to put it down to the scare he had given me.

"Jenny."

The way he said my name, softly as though he were trying it out for the first time, sent shivers down my spine. Oh, God, no, I thought. Not again. Please let me be over him. I shut my eyes for a moment. I felt as though I had been dropped into the middle of a whirlpool that was threatening to drag me under. The claustrophobic sensation of drowning swept over me, competing with a wild feeling of excitement and dread.

Bruce grinned at me and swept his hand through my hair, saying my name over again.

"What did you want, Bruce?" I forced myself to be businesslike.

He sighed. "Ah, Jenny. I knew when I saw you last night that it was the answer to everything. Carole's no good for me. I never should have married her." He rubbed his hands along my shoulders. "She's had everything her way for so long. The way she's been carrying on with Geoff. Oh, she's clever about it, I'll say that for her, but I know. She wanted my money, and now thanks to King I'm not good enough for her. I've been such a fool all these years, stuck with Carole. It's taken your coming back to make me see it. It's going to be us again, Jenny. Somehow I've always known you'd come back to me."

I was angry with him, momentarily, for taking me for granted. Then my anger turned to anxiety. I wasn't ready for Bruce yet.

I reached up and took his hands from my shoulders. "This isn't the time for that, Bruce. Elizabeth expects us for dinner in half an hour. I've been gone all day. I have to shower and change."

Surprisingly, he was agreeable. "Okay. Meet me here after dinner. It'll be dark then. Say about nine."

His hand brushed my cheek, and before I could reply he had slipped into the trees.

I walked back up the path, my head down, my mind on Bruce. I didn't hear Carole until I had nearly run into her. She stopped in the middle of the path, blocking my way. Suspicion sharpened her voice.

"Where's Bruce?"

"Down by the falls." Too late I realized my answer was a give-away that I had been with him.

"Stay away from him, Jenny." She was angry. Whether it was real or feigned, I didn't know.

"I don't have to account to you for what I do, Carole," I told her coldly.

"I'm warning you. If you know what's good for you, you'll stay away from Bruce."

"You're being melodramatic, Carole. If you want him so badly, I suggest you go find him. I'm going to the Castle." I swept past her and left her standing on the path.

———◆———

We gathered for dinner promptly at seven and for a while I thought it was going to be a repeat of the night before. Bruce clearly wanted to monopolize me, but Carole hung onto him so ardently that he couldn't. Paul and Lynn stood together, sipping their drinks. King and Elizabeth strained to entertain me, while Geoffrey stood aloof, dark and brooding in the middle of a house filled with false gaiety. I downed two martinis and felt that I was ready to face the evening.

As we sat down Lynn asked brightly, "How was your day, Jenny?"

"Fine. It's great country. I hadn't realized how much I missed it."

"Then perhaps you'll stay with us," King suggested.

I smiled, mentally noting that Christopher was watching me intently. "I'm afraid you don't have any airports here that need administrative personnel."

"I'm sure there's something we could find for you to do," Elizabeth joined in.

"If she sells to Greenberg, she won't need to work," Paul reminded.

"Ah, yes," King muttered, pushing his soup bowl away and leaning his elbows on the table. I saw Elizabeth frown, but she said nothing. "Greenberg. What way are you leaning, Jenny, or do you prefer we mind our own business?"

I retained my smile, but underneath I was wary. I felt as though he were baiting me. "I really don't know," I replied easily. "I haven't even talked to him."

"What did you do today?" Elizabeth seemed to want to turn the conversation away from the topic of the ski area. I willingly obliged.

"I took care of some of Father's affairs. Then I drove up Cottonwood and walked around for a bit until I met Christopher. I spent the rest of the day boring him with tales of my childhood."

"Sounds as though you had a pleasant time," Lynn commented as she cleared the table for the main course. "I'm glad you managed to corral Chris for a while. He spends too much time alone."

"I'm sure he didn't appreciate your stories of us growing up the way I would have, Jenny. Next time you want to reminisce let me know." Bruce flashed a conspiratorial smile at me.

"I doubt that she wants your company, Bruce." Carole was pulling too tightly on the strings. That was a sure way to lose Bruce, as I well knew. Despite her warning, I wondered if she cared. Sarah Gibson had mentioned something about Carole and Geoff and so had Bruce. I took a long drink of wine. Perhaps Carole was pretending to be the jealous wife to drive us together. Then she would be free for Geoff. It made sense.

"Just because you're tired of me, Carole, it doesn't mean everyone else is." Bruce slid smoothly out of her net, jabbing at her while he was doing it. Clearly they were masters at the art of polite hostility.

King frowned disapprovingly and paused as he was carving the roast. He didn't seem to like the hostile bickering. Elizabeth, on the other hand, serenely ignored it.

"Actually," I said trying to pick up the thread of the conversation, ignoring Bruce. "It wasn't all as quiet a time as I've made it sound. We had a couple of very exciting moments." I thought Lynn stiffened a little at that, and I watched her closely. By innocently recounting what had happened, I might be able to learn something from the various reactions.

"Really?" Elizabeth took my bait, politely. "Exciting in what way?"

"We were sitting in the middle of a large talus pile and somehow a rather large boulder from the top of the slide must have gotten undermined from our tramping around. It came roaring down on us and, if it hadn't been for Christopher's sharp ears, we both could have been badly hurt. As it was, we got out of the way, but I must admit that I was pretty scared for a few seconds." I tried to sound casual about it.

I got my reactions. Paul and Lynn exchanged quick, worried glances and I heard Lynn swallow an exclamation. Christopher shot me a hurt, angry look, while Geoffrey calmly continued eating, not deigning to look up. King and Elizabeth expressed their concern.

"We've told Christopher often enough about these slides," King said. "They can be treacherous."

"So he told me. It wasn't his fault," I assured them, not wanting to get the boy into trouble with my little ploy.

Carole seemed amused. Bruce seized upon the incident as a pretext to issue another proposal. "You see, Jenny. You need someone to protect you. Next time you're thirsting for an expedition I'll serve as your guide."

My reaction was automatic. "Christopher did quite admirably. Next time, I'll take his advice."

Bruce smiled affably as though he thought my reply was a blind put on for Carole's benefit. Surprisingly, it was this that brought a response of sorts from Geoffrey. I glanced over and found him looking at me somberly. Our eyes caught for a second, and then he dropped his to the coffee he was stirring. He's a cold-blooded bastard, I thought. He didn't seem to care about his son.

Elizabeth steered the conversation on and, surprisingly, the rest of dinner passed quickly and easily. As we were finishing our chocolate mousse, King again turned to me. "What are your plans for tomorrow, Jenny?"

"I haven't decided really."

"We're going to go on a long ride," Bruce interposed. "I'll show you country I bet you've forgotten."

"I'm afraid I couldn't ride a horse that long. I'm terribly out of practice as Paul can testify from this morning."

"Then we'll take the jeep."

"In that case, I think I'll come along," Carole interposed lazily. "A day in the mountains is just what I need."

Oh my God, I thought. How was I going to get out of this? If there was one thing I didn't want to do it was spend a day with Bruce and Carole. I wasn't even sure at this point that I wanted to spend a day with Bruce. King sensed my predicament.

"Why don't you make a party out of it. Geoff, you can take the day off and go too. Besides, I'd feel better if I knew you were driving."

Nothing registered on Geoffrey's implacable face. He nodded

briefly. Angrily, Bruce started to speak and then apparently thought the better of it. It was evident that he wasn't happy with the turn of events.

"How about you, Lynn?" I asked.

"Afraid not. Four people are all that fit comfortably in a jeep."

"You could take the other one," Elizabeth suggested.

"No." Lynn was firm. "I have to help Paul in the office tomorrow. His girl wanted a day off." She said it smoothly enough, but somehow I knew that it was an excuse. I wondered why.

"Well, we've a party then," Carole said, reaching for the coffeepot. "How cozy."

It would be a dreadful day, I thought. I could tell already.

———◆———

I was undecided about meeting Bruce. He had been annoying at dinner. I disliked his smooth certainty that I would fall at his feet again. But I was angry with myself for running away from him earlier. Sternly, I told myself that I was mature enough to face him and see how I felt about him. So at nine, I let myself out the front door and took the path that led to the base of Rob Roy Falls. Bruce wasn't there so I lit a cigarette and prepared myself for this second encounter. I had smoked three cigarettes and was getting ready to leave when I heard him coming up behind me.

"Jenny." He put his hands on my shoulders and as I turned to face him, he bent his head and kissed me.

He was his old suave, assured self; the Bruce I had been wild about when I was nineteen. Once my heart had raced when Bruce embraced me. Now it beat erratically. I broke out of his arms, afraid of my response.

He smiled amusedly. "Come on now, Jenny." He reached out and playfully ruffled my hair. He had done the same thing earlier, I remembered. He moved toward me. I stepped back a couple of paces and managed to get a cigarette out of my pocket. I lit it, trying to put the frail glowing weed between us. I drew the smoke into my lungs.

"You took your time. I was getting ready to leave."

"I was here. I was watching you."

I wasn't sure that I liked that, and I told him so.

"Don't be so touchy, Jenny," he countered smoothly.

It was twilight and the darkness was encroaching quickly. I couldn't see his face clearly anymore. There was a big rock by the side of the path. I leaned against it. "What was so important that you had to get me down here?"

"I wanted to be alone with you."

"I'm touched," I told him with a trace of irony. I was trying to defend myself against Bruce with bitchiness.

He didn't notice. "Don't let Carole bother you. She's going to be nasty. That's just something we're going to have to live with."

He took the cigarette out of my fingers and threw it on the ground. I watched him as though I were a third person carefully observing what was going to happen to a puppet named Jenifer. This time when he kissed me I was oppressed by a sense of unreality.

It was Bruce who broke this embrace. He was annoyed but he kept control. "You certainly aren't very responsive. You used to do better. Much better. What's the matter?"

I couldn't let Bruce see my inner confusion. I gave him a general answer that was true but imprecise. "What happened between us was a long time ago, Bruce. People change. We can't go back to that."

He seemed relieved. "Is that all." He caught my hand and held it tightly. "I know it's been a while, Jen, but we'll start again. Both of us. It will be better this time." He was radiating confidence. He smiled at me rakishly. He started to lean toward me again, but Carole's voice calling his name stopped him.

An angry grimace crossed his face. "I'd better go back," he said. "Carole's looking for me and there's no sense in having a scene now. Tomorrow we'll talk about us." He slipped off into the darkness before I could say anything.

Left alone, I leaned against the rock and looked down the Box as the last vestiges of light faded into the Utah desert a hundred miles away, making the western skyline a delicate pink. I still didn't know how I felt about Bruce. Meeting him had solved nothing. On the one hand, I was still attracted to him, to his easy, smooth charm and the way he made me feel special, wanted, desired. On the other hand, I disliked his cocksure manner, his certainty that I would fall into his arms again. I fought against getting involved with him again. It would be so easy to do. And yet, even if I wanted to—and I wasn't sure that I did—I knew it was useless. Carole had meant what she'd said. She would never give him up.

I stayed by the falls for a long time. It grew dark and the lights of Kingsville began to glitter in the alpine air. The moon came out, casting a surrealistic radiance over the Box, and I gazed up to find Venus looking so close that it seemed I could reach up and grab it. I thought of making a wish, but I didn't know what to wish for.

"Good evening, Jenny. Is anything the matter?"

I lurched. The moonlight was on my face, and I realized that for the second time that day I had been caught with tears on my lashes. I hadn't minded Christopher so much, but Geoff was another matter. This time I really did feel like a fool. I brushed the tears away and turned my head slowly to look at him. "No," I said, finally, in a muted tone. "Everything's fine."

He looked at me as though he didn't believe it, but he didn't say anything. He took a pack of cigarettes out of his pocket and offered me one. I drew it out of the pack and bent down to the match he held cupped in his hands. I moved over slightly so that he could lean against the rock and we stood, silently smoking. Neither of us felt much like talking. Finally, Geoff flicked his cigarette on the path and ground it out with his heel.

"Carole's out after your scalp you know," he commented nonchalantly. "She can be pretty vicious when she wants."

I glanced at him. "I'm sure she can, but how does it concern you?" I hadn't meant to sound hostile, but I knew it had come out that way.

"Let's just say I don't like to see lambs slaughtered."

"I can take care of myself," I assured him a bit testily.

"Can you?" The tone of his voice hadn't changed, but I knew that he didn't believe I was much of a match for his sister-in-law.

I didn't much care whether he thought I could cope with Carole. His comment had reminded me of Christopher.

"If you're so concerned about lambs, I'd think you'd pay a bit more attention to your son," I challenged him.

"Why? Because of your little scare on the talus this afternoon?"

"Yes. He could have been badly hurt."

He shrugged disinterestedly. "He wasn't."

"You could have shown some concern anyway."

"There was no reason to." He was cold.

I was angry suddenly. "There's every reason," I insisted.

"I don't really think it's any affair of yours."

I knew he had meant his chilly rejoinder to cut off discussion on the matter, but I persisted. "For God's sake," I began. I stopped. My tone was all wrong. Where I should have been firm, I was pleading. It wouldn't work on a man like Geoffrey Cabot and I knew it. "He's just a child. He needs to know that his father cares about him. That is," I added darkly, "if you do."

I could see his sardonic smile. I knew that, if there were enough light, his blue eyes would be as icy and cold as frozen tundra. Still his tone didn't vary. "For someone who can't run her own life very well, you seem to be good at giving advice."

My reaction was instinctive. I slapped him. His head rocked back, but other than that he didn't move. "And you're about the rudest man I've ever met." My voice was shaking with anger. I felt, more than saw, him looking at me, and I sensed the same tension between us that I had noticed in my hotel room earlier.

He moved away from the rock and took a few steps back up the path. "Good night, Jenifer." He was overly polite.

I felt as though a bucket of ice water had been thrown over me. I didn't know why Geoffrey brought out the worst in me— my insecurity and my hostility. I waited until I was sure I wouldn't accidentally run into him, and then I went back to the

Castle. It had been an exhausting day and I was more then ready for bed.

I was half-asleep when I heard the soft knocking on my door. I groaned, got up, flicked on the light, then stumbled over to the door and opened it.

It was Christopher. Instantly I was awake.

"I couldn't sleep," he explained as he came inside the room and stood there, warily glancing around.

"What is it? Can I help?"

He was quiet for a moment, and then the words burst from him. "You said you wanted to be my friend. Why did you tell them?"

"You've never told any of them about the other times, have you? How many have there been?"

"Three," he replied reluctantly.

"And you think you know who it is. That's why you didn't want me to say anything about meeting you on top of Rob Roy Falls that day. You were afraid he'd think I'd seen him."

Again he nodded. He was clearly miserable. I led him over to the bed and we sat down. I put my arm around him. Who, I wondered, did he think was responsible? Then, suddenly, I guessed.

"You think it's your father, don't you?"

He stared at the floor, his shoulders slumped. "It's always his horse," he said tonelessly. "The sorrel. And the rider wears his hat."

"Someone else could have picked it up and worn it."

"No. He always has it." He insisted on the point stubbornly.

"But why would he want to hurt you? It doesn't make sense. You're his son."

"He hates me," the boy said simply. "Because of my mother."

I bit my lip. I was in as much agony as he was. At that moment I could have murdered Geoffrey Cabot myself. I was only sorry that I hadn't hit him harder.

"I tried to run away once, but Aunt Lynn caught me and

brought me back. Now she watches me. She's careful about it, but I know she's there. When you go, would you take me with you?" He looked at me anxiously. The dark lashes swept up revealing his extraordinarily blue eyes—the Cabot eyes. "I don't mean you have to look after me. Just help me get away."

I tried to refuse his request gently. "I can't promise you anything, Chris. I'll try to help you in whatever way I can. Maybe you should tell your Aunt Lynn what's been going on," I suggested.

"No." He was violent about it.

At last I understood all of it. "You're trying to protect your father, aren't you? You must love him very much."

He just looked at me with his father's eyes.

"All right, Chris." I drew him closer to me. "You can trust me. We're in this together."

He accepted that and started to get up, but seemed a bit uncertain. On impulse, I asked him if he would like to stay. He nodded tenuously and crawled under the covers. He went to sleep nestled in my arms.

CHAPTER 5

Lynn was the first one I saw when I came downstairs the next morning. I was sorry that circumstances would prevent my talking to her today. I had the feeling that we were both desperately trying to avoid the inevitable confrontation.

Breakfast at Castle Cabot was an informal affair. I greeted her cheerily and found a plate, helping myself to sausage, steak and eggs. Normally I didn't eat in the morning, but the mountain air had changed that.

Lynn paused momentarily, then continued buttering her toast. "I trust you slept well last night despite the disturbance."

I turned to look at her. "I didn't hear a thing."

A grimace twisted her mouth into an ugly thin-lipped smile. "You didn't miss much."

"What happened?"

She was reluctant to tell me for a moment. I could see her deciding, weighing the possibilities in her mind. At last she said, "Just Bruce and Carole. Another screaming argument. You're lucky you're at the other end of the hall. You're in for a jolly day. I don't envy you."

I wasn't about to tell her that I shared her misgivings, so I let her comment pass. I finished heaping my plate, took a deep breath and went into the dining room.

They were all there, seated around the big table, when I entered. Bruce had his back toward me, but he must have been listening for the door. He jumped up immediately. "Jenny. Good morning." He pulled back my chair and leaned toward me to kiss my cheek. "Hope you slept well in spite of Carole's vocal exercises. She was a bit distraught last night."

Once again I wasn't sure that I liked being claimed so blatantly. I moved away from Bruce slightly, putting my plate on the table and reaching for the coffeepot. I smiled at him noncommittally. "Good morning all. Sorry to be late. I haven't quite adjusted my internal time clock yet." I slipped into the chair. "And here I am starving again. If I don't watch out, I'm going to go back to San Francisco twenty pounds heavier." I plunged into the steak hoping that I wouldn't have to carry on much of a conversation while I was eating.

I half-expected Carole to make some biting remark about Bruce's greeting, but she was strangely silent. I wondered if she and Bruce had settled things between themselves, or if she was merely biding her time, waiting until we were away from King and Elizabeth. Neither of them liked her bickering with Bruce, and I felt that she wanted to stay in their good graces.

Bruce kept trying to get me to talk. "We've got a great day for a trip," he commented. "With a little luck, we won't even run into an afternoon storm. Where would you like to go, Jenny?"

"I thought you would have had it all mapped out by now."

"No. I insisted we wait until you came down. I wanted to make sure we consulted your preferences." He was making a great show of his devoted attention to me. I could feel the silent hostility radiating from Carole and, glancing quickly sideways, I saw Elizabeth's speculative gaze fixed upon her son.

"No preferences." I picked up the salt shaker and concentrated on my breakfast.

Carole's fingers drummed a heavy staccato on the table. "You'd better decide, Bruce, since Jenny has such an open mind." She was sweet, but I caught the deadly venom behind her amiability.

Bruce seemed pleased that the choice was left up to him. "I thought we'd go up Red Canyon and over into Ouray. Then we can go down to the Galena road and drop back into Mithral Basin and down the escarpment." It sounded simple enough, but I knew that it would take all day.

"We can investigate some of the old dumps in the Mithral Basin and stop at that little cabin. Remember it, Jen?"

I would never forget it, but I wasn't about to admit that to Bruce. It had been the place we had gone that summer when we wanted to be alone, and it was there that Bruce had made love to me the first time. Oh, yes, I remembered it. Probably better than he.

I took a long sip of coffee. "Yes, I know the cabin you mean." My tone was so matter-of-fact that even I was astounded.

King put down his paper. "That's a long trip. I don't want you coming down the escarpment in the dark, so you'd better get started. Geoff, I'm counting on you to keep these other three from falling off cliffs and into mine shafts." What he really meant was that he counted on Geoff to keep us from each others' throats. I wondered for a moment that he seemed to trust Geoffrey more than he did his own son. In many ways Geoffrey was so much more competent and reliable than Bruce who had never overcome being the spoiled Prince Charming. It was just those qualities in Geoff, however, that made him so suspect. I remembered Christopher's face when he had come to my room. Most of all I couldn't trust Geoffrey Cabot. Lynn had been right. It was going to be a bitch of a day.

Bruce and I piled into the narrow back seat of the jeep. Most of the right hand side was taken up by Elizabeth's generous lunch, so I had no choice but to sit uncomfortably close to him. Leisurely, Carole climbed into the front. Geoff drove.

Carole touched his shoulder. "You can explain all the rock formations to me, Geoff darling. And you," she continued turning to smile frostily at Bruce, "can point out all the aesthetic sights."

Bruce put his arm around my shoulders and pulled me closer to him. "Everything's all settled, darling," he whispered in my ear. "It's going to be you and me from now on."

"Is it?" I hadn't looked at him yet. A night's sleep hadn't made me any more decisive about Bruce. I was still torn, unable to come to grips with what I wanted. All I knew for certain was that I wasn't as immune to his charms as I told myself I wanted to be.

"Sure. Carole will be nasty for a while, but she'll just have to learn that when I want something I go after it. I told her that last night." He was so sure of himself. And not only he, I realized, but all of them. They all expected me to fall into Bruce's arms again. I half-expected it myself. Sitting close to him I could feel some of the old tug at my emotions. I drifted with it for a moment, leaning toward him, caught by his confident magnetism. Then I stopped myself. No. I wasn't a poor, insecure, love-sick girl any longer. I was a mature woman, capable, competent.

"Besides," Bruce was saying, "she really wants Geoff. Just look." He nodded toward Carole who was stroking the back of Geoff's neck with her supple, expressive fingers. "Not that she can get him," Bruce added with some satisfaction. "We'll get away from them once we get to the Basin. I knew you'd remember that cabin. We had some good times there." His arm tightened around me and I could feel the passion rising in him. I knew that he intended to seduce me once we got to the cabin.

I forestalled his passionate declaration. "We'll talk later, Bruce. This isn't the place."

He accepted that and I settled back, trying to ignore him, concentrating on the unending beauty of the San Juans. Geoff drove expertly, piloting the jeep along the narrow, winding road that snaked its way up the side of Red Canyon. The road climbed steadily and in an hour we were up about 11,000 feet with cliffs of carmine-red granite on the left and a dizzying thousand-foot drop on the right. A hairpin curve brought us to a thin ribbon of water that plummeted over the road, spattering briefly on the smooth rocks. Geoff stayed to the inside of the curve so that we were behind the waterfall, and I looked up to see the spray of water beginning to catch the morning sun.

It was another hour before we rounded the switchback that took us out of Red Canyon and through a rock arch into a large basin. Bruce and I talked occasionally, mostly about the scenery or remembering things we had done in our childhood. I relaxed a little. He was being good company. I had to lean close to him to hear over the roar of the jeep motor. Twice he started to caress me and I pulled away, uneasy, trapped between my temptation to give in to him and my determination not to let him hurt me again. I would be tense for a while and then I would be lulled into lowering my guard.

Close to noon Geoff stopped the jeep beside a small lake formed from the melting snow. So far the trip hadn't been as bad as I'd anticipated, but now I knew that the peacefulness would be shattered. I tensed myself for the inevitable confrontation. I didn't have long to wait.

"Well, Jenny," Carole turned to face us. "I trust my husband was properly attentive and pointed out all the scenic attractions." Bruce still had his arm around me, and, although she didn't say anything, I saw her eyes harden.

"I enjoyed the ride," I told her evenly.

She flipped her long blond hair carelessly with one hand. "I bet you did."

"How about some lunch." Geoff slid easily out of the jeep and reached for one of the wicker baskets.

"Good idea." Bruce leaped over the side of the jeep and held out his hand to me. I chose to ignore it.

Carole laughed harshly. "Try again, darling. Maybe our Jenifer's far-sighted."

I moved out of the line of fire, but it did little good. They kept sniping at each other throughout lunch, each unable to stop for fear the other had gotten the upper hand. When Carole's comments weren't directed toward Bruce, she aimed them at me. Bruce insisted on keeping me beside him, lavishing attention on me. I accepted it for a while, but with reservations. Geoff sat off to one side, skipping rocks in the lake, trying to ignore the rest of us. Gradually, Carole grew more and more vicious and Bruce's temper began to deteriorate.

At last Bruce attempted to silence her. "You may as well give up, Carole. Nothing you can say will do any good. I told you last night that I've made up my mind and nothing is going to change it. Lay off." He delivered his ultimatum a bit too sulkily to be effective.

Carole laughed mirthlessly. She knew her husband well. "'I've made up my mind,'" she mimicked. "It's going to take more than that, Bruce. I told Jenny I wasn't going to let you go, and I meant it. Play around with her if you want, although I can't see why you'd want to, but I'll never let you go any farther than that. Both of you better realize that."

I had had enough. I was fed up with being treated like a fresh dog bone. I felt that I was merely a pretext for the two of them to fight. Neither of them cared about me or how I felt. They were simply using me in their never-ending battle, and I didn't like it. I stood up, shaking off Bruce's detaining hand.

"What's the matter, Jenny? Going to cut and run? You never could take it could you?"

I stared at Carole coldly. "You're both disgusting. I'm going for a walk." I stalked around the lake and began to climb the steeply pitched slope that led to the top of a nearby mountain. I was shaking with anger, mostly at myself for being unable to settle my feelings about Bruce. I disliked him, I realized. Or at least I disliked him when he was sulking and pouting. I resented him when he took me for granted. I was angry that despite that, I still felt attracted to him.

Berating myself, I attacked the mountain vigorously. After climbing several hundred feet, I had to stop to catch my breath. The mountain air was painfully thin and my lungs sucked greedily at the oxygen I inhaled in great gulps. A few moments later I pushed on, but this time I was able to go only about a hundred feet before I was forced to stop again. My legs felt like leaden hunks attached to my body and I was breathing heavily. I was certainly not in condition for this sort of thing.

I was ready to start out again when Geoff caught up with me. "Thought I'd join you," he said while inhaling deeply. "Hope you don't mind."

"Suit yourself," I told him shortly.

"Sorry it's me and not Bruce," he baited me.

So it was his turn now. "To hell with every goddamn one of you Cabots," I exploded. I left him with that, resuming the climb.

My outburst silenced him for he said nothing more, but he matched me step for step, waiting patiently while I stopped to replenish my energy. I wondered why, since he was in much better condition than I and could have easily outdistanced me. After a grueling forty-five minutes we reached the top. The exertion of the climb had dissipated my anger, and I was able to sit, trying to regain my perspective. The crumpled white and steel-blue mass of the San Juans was spread out before me, running in every direction, stretching into infinity, wild and remote—each jagged peak some primeval Valhalla.

I turned to Geoff who was sitting a few feet from me, chewing speculatively on a blade of grass. "Feel better now?" he asked casually.

I shrugged. "I suppose so." I refused to apologize for my bad humor.

"I told you Carole could be vicious," he said. "That was just a sample." He seemed to be warning me.

Our gazes locked for a moment, and once again I could feel that odd tension that seemed to run between us. Looking at him —somber, darkly handsome in a blue pullover knit shirt that was partially open—I remembered Christopher. Selfishly, I had been thinking of myself.

"Geoff." His eyes narrowed sharply as he detected the change in my tone. "I want to talk to you."

Suddenly the distance between us was immense. I felt him stiffen. It was as though a portcullis had thudded down, cutting him off from me.

"It's about Christopher . . ."

"We settled that last night." He was curt, almost rude.

"No. We didn't. I know you think it's none of my business and technically you have a point, but someone has to talk to you. Christopher came to my room last night. He had no one else to turn to. He's afraid of you. He wants so much to have you notice him, pay attention to him." With an effort I kept the emotion out of my voice. I had to be matter-of-fact about this or I would never reach him.

"You're absolutely right. It's none of your affair." He was slightly irritated now.

"I know how he feels," I persisted doggedly, "wanting to have his father care about him. It can warp him, scar him emotionally, for the rest of his life. Believe me. I know what I'm talking about." I shuddered. I had done what I had wanted to avoid.

"I'm sure you think you do." He was polite but annoyed. "I can only repeat that it's no concern of yours."

"I'm making it my concern."

He became ice cold. "Look, Jenifer, I've tried to be nice about this. Now I don't want to hear anything more about it. If you have any sense, you'll get out of the Castle and leave the Cabots to themselves," he finished darkly.

Imperious bastard, I thought. "For God's sake," I blazed, "stop being such a bloody piece of granite! He's your son! You of all people should know what it's like to be shut out. I know Elizabeth must have hurt you terribly, but how can you do the same thing to Christopher. He's a fine, intelligent, sensitive boy. He's so alone, so frightened—and he loves you." My plea trailed off lamely. What was the use of talking to this man about love. I doubted if he had ever cared about another human being. I wondered why he had even bothered to get married.

I could see his jaw tightening and I knew I was in for it. "Neither I, nor my son, need you muddling around in our lives . . ."

"Speak for yourself," I cut in. "Not for your son. You don't even know him. That's the whole problem. Just because your wife left you, don't take it out on Christopher."

He stood at that and stepped over to tower above me. His teeth were clenched tightly and a muscle in his jaw twitched spasmodically. "Don't ever mention my wife to me again." He ground it out between his teeth.

I stood up to face him, staring straight into his angry blue eyes, glowing now like bits of blue fire. "Somebody's got to. So she left you. You've still got Christopher."

He raised his hand as though he were going to strike me. I

stood my ground and braced myself for the blow, but instead he turned abruptly and walked several paces away from me. I waited a moment and then followed him. I was a bit shaken to discover not only the passionate anger I had roused in him but also his iron-clad control. Even then, he hadn't lost it. He stood pounding his fist into the palm of his other hand. The sharp sounds echoed in the clear air.

"I almost hit you," he said strangely.

"Yes." I was calm again, my anger broken. Once again I met his gaze, and we stood locked in an intense, unknown world of our own. I wondered fleetingly if I was crazy baiting a man I thought to be a murderer, or at least a would-be murderer. And where did I choose to do it but atop this craggy wilderness where it would be so easy to kill someone. A little shove was all it would take, and no one would ever be the wiser. He still held my eyes. I felt drained, as if he were devouring me with his icy blue stare, but I wasn't about to drop my gaze.

I saw my hand move to touch his arm, and I knew what I was going to say. I didn't know why and chances were that I would regret it, but some instinct led me to take the gamble. If he were indeed a murderer, I was placing my life between him and Christopher.

"Geoff, don't you see what's happening. That falling boulder wasn't an accident. Someone is trying to kill the boy. Why, I don't know. Who, I don't know. But yesterday wasn't the first time. He's scared to death because he thinks it's you. He's tried running away, but Lynn brings him back. He even wanted me to take him to San Francisco. Geoff, you've got to help him."

A new look came into his eyes. I couldn't define it, but at last he seemed interested. "How do you know this?" He asked the question with an intensity that surprised me.

I told him about my first meeting with Christopher, then about finding the crowbar marks and horse tracks above the talus. I knew I was being ten times a fool, but I went on unheeding.

Geoff listened attentively. "So he thinks I'm trying to kill him," he remarked in a strained tone when I had finished. "Did he tell you why?"

I nodded. Here we go again, I thought. "Because of your wife. He thinks you hate him." I waited for his anger, but it didn't come.

"My God," he said absently. Then he laughed unpleasantly. "Aren't you taking a chance, Jenny? Maybe he's right." His eyes narrowed into his old hooded look, and I was suddenly afraid of him.

A queer silence hung between us. I continued to gaze at him openly, studying him, refusing to betray my fear. Finally, I took a deep breath and answered him. "Maybe you are," I agreed steadily. "Everything certainly points to it. Lord knows you're cold-hearted enough, but—" I searched for the explanation for my foolishness. "You were always the one who took in the birds with the broken wings and sprung the leg traps that you'd find in the mountains." I dropped my head and stared at the ground. A slight wind had sprung up, blowing through my hair and gently whipping at the back of my shirt. "I don't know, Geoff," I finished lamely, "but I seem to have taken the gamble that you're not a killer."

He turned away and was silent for a long time. Finally, he spoke without looking at me. "All right, Jenny. I don't know what good it will do, but I'll try to pay more attention to the boy." He turned to face me then. "I underestimated you. You're a hell of a lot tougher than you used to be."

We came off the mountain more quickly than we had ascended. Twice I slipped on flat pieces of slide rock and each time Geoff caught me, steadying me with his arm. I dismissed the unsettling feeling that went through me at his touch.

Carole saw us first. She was leaning nonchalantly against the side of the jeep, looking like some sort of feline waiting for her prey. Framed against the background of the basin she could have been a Hollywood model doing an advertisement for Lady Manhattan shirts or some little cigar. She really was breathtakingly lovely, I thought. It was depressing to be average looking. There was nothing so damning as mediocrity.

"Well," she greeted us, looking up from her inspection of her long polished nails, "you certainly took your time." The bitter, taunting venom she had displayed at lunch was completely gone and instead she was calm, triumphant. Again the cat image popped into my mind and I had a fantasy of her serenely licking her paws. Bruce must have come out on the short end of the battle.

A look at him confirmed my guess. He was haggard, his eyes a bit sunken. There was a resentful, hangdog look about him that I didn't care for. "Glad you're back. We should get going, Geoff, if we're going to make the circle." He avoided looking at me.

Geoff nodded, picked up the two picnic baskets and carefully arranged them in the back of the jeep.

"Poor Geoffrey," Carole laughed merrily. "You know we used to think he was a deaf mute because he never talked." She moved around behind him, reaching up to muss his hair as she passed. She was definitely feeling good. Geoff smoothed his hair back in place. "He's just antisocial," Carole continued. "Could you get him to talk at all, Jenny?"

I ignored her.

"Don't tell me you're antisocial too, Jenny. What a lovely couple." She let the suggestion hang in the air, for whose benefit I didn't know.

"I only talk to people I like," I said curtly.

She had no reply. Climbing into the back seat she held out her hand to Bruce. He followed her, deliberately avoiding my gaze.

I was mystified. Slowly, I swung into the front seat of the jeep and admitted that I had no idea how to explain their change in behavior, let alone the dynamics of their relationship. Did they want each other or not? I had no answer. Whatever his desire, the nets had closed back over Bruce. In a way I was relieved. It saved me from having to come to terms with my conflicting feelings.

We dropped down on the eastern side of the San Juans, drove through Ouray and then cut back west again on the old Galena road. Galena was another term for lead ore, I remembered, and one of the oldest of the Colvada Mining Company's holdings was a lead mine perched high on the eastern slope of the mountains. The road was wider than most and in good condition. It wound laboriously up the sides of canyons, over ridges, through forests and over great open meadows. Occasionally, we would meet a huge yellow Mack truck with a big black CMC blazoned on its door barreling down the precipitous road with all the confidence bred of familiarity.

We passed the Galena finally and soon came over the pass that led to Mithral Basin. Geoff drove by the cabin that had been Bruce's special place to take me that long ago summer. He didn't stop and Bruce didn't protest. I was glad not to have to face another difficult scene.

None of us talked much. I could sometimes hear a murmur from the back indicating that Bruce and Carole were still talking to one another, and whenever we had to stop to let another jeep pass, Geoff would politely explain some of the geologic formations and point out the various peaks. I was foolishly pleased that he had voluntarily decided to be my guide. I still didn't know if I trusted him, but it was nice to show Carole that her taciturn brother-in-law would talk to me when he had said hardly anything to her. Spiteful, I told myself, but decidedly pleasant nevertheless.

It wasn't until our last halt, near the top of the escarpment, that I finally admitted that there was something unsettling about those moments as well. When we were moving, when I was busy absorbing the changing scenes and my thoughts were drowned out by the low growl of the jeep's motor, I could ignore it. But when we were stopped, I was distinctly—almost uncomfortably —aware of Geoffrey Cabot's cold, hard, brooding personality.

———◆———

Lynn and Christopher were sitting on the front steps when we got back to the Castle. Carole got out of the jeep and tugged at Bruce's arm, "Come on, darling. Let's go have a drink. I'm dry after that long ride."

Bruce looked at me briefly, then took Carole's hand and they walked past Lynn and Christopher into the house. Lynn watched them for a moment, then she stood up leisurely, turning her attention to Geoffrey and me. Geoff had swung the two picnic baskets out of the jeep and was starting toward the steps. I put my hand on his arm, stopping him.

"Geoff." I said it much more firmly than I felt.

He didn't speak but the left corner of his mouth moved slightly in annoyance and then he sighed so softly that I thought I might have imagined it. "All right, Jenny, all right."

I dropped my hand and let him go, waiting apprehensively to see what he would do. He strode lightly up the first two steps until he was beside Christopher. The boy, very small and forlorn sitting beneath his father's towering form, was quietly looking at me standing in the driveway.

"Christopher." Geoff's voice was noticeably loud. He's as uncertain of himself as I am, I thought.

Christopher looked up at him.

"How would you like to help me with these baskets?"

I could sense Christopher's fear and doubt. If only Geoff would see it. Chris took the basket and trudged up the steps, following his father.

Lynn was frowning as she turned to me. "Odd," I heard her murmur under her breath. "Well, Jenny," she said aloud in that cool, businesslike tone I was coming to know well. "I'm glad to see you in one piece."

"I didn't expect not to be."

Lynn hesitated as though she were making up her mind about something. I stepped past her and started toward the Castle when she said, "Jenny, let's go down to Mithral Falls. We need to have a talk."

I turned. She was standing beside the jeep looking cool, refreshed, competent—all the things I was lacking after the long day. It wasn't the moment I would have picked for a talk with Lynn, but it would have to do. "If you want," I agreed, wondering what she had in mind.

She led the way to a path I had almost forgotten which cut off to the left of the Castle, ending abruptly near Mithral Falls. There were a few Douglas fir beside the path and some low scrubby growth of juniper. Their scents crossed and mingled with a pungent sweetness. I caught the low, throaty croak of a frog and the high chirping of the army of crickets that appeared each evening in the mountains. Lynn kept walking until she reached the pile of rocks that marked the end of the trail. She leaned casually against them, one foot tucked up behind her, her arms folded. I found a fair-sized rock, sat down and looked at her expectantly.

She was staring at the ground, her long auburn hair falling over her face. Her voice was carefully controlled and, I thought, a little subdued. "I apologize for letting you go today without trying to make you see what was going to happen. I could tell that Carole has Bruce in line again." She shook the hair out of her eyes and looked at me with that Cabot gaze, a smaller, feminine version of Geoff's.

"It seems so," I agreed serenely.

"That doesn't seem to bother you." It was a statement, but the question lay underneath and I sensed a kind of tension in her as she waited for my reply.

"Why don't you stop beating around the bush, Lynn. It's unlike you. What is it you want to know?"

She looked vaguely uncomfortable and shifted position, tucking her other leg behind her this time. "In a sense it's none of my business, but—what are you going to do about Bruce?"

"Do?" I echoed. "Nothing probably."

Her brows came together in a deep frown. "I'm not sure I understand you."

I smiled ruefully. "I'm sure you don't. I don't think I understand it either. When I came back I didn't know whether I was still in love with Bruce. I'm still not sure. He's a very attractive man and it's difficult not to respond to him. It's all a moot question anyway," I went on briskly. "He's not strong enough to break away from Carole, even if he really wanted to. So you don't have to worry about your brother. I'll be leaving in a week or so, and he'll forget all about me again—the way he did before."

As I said it I realized that Lynn had forced me to come to terms with some of my feelings. I had become practical, and I had been holding myself away from Bruce's magnetism because I knew it wouldn't work. It would have been easy to have an affair with him, but I wanted more than that. I wanted a relationship built on something solid and positive, and I wasn't sure Bruce could give it to me.

Lynn was silent for a while looking down at her hands, twisting the ring around her finger as if she didn't know quite what to say to me. When she spoke her tone was warmer. "You *have* changed, Jenny. I'm concerned about you, not Bruce. He's always been selfish, spoiled; always wanted the easy way out. You never saw it ten years ago, but it was there and it's gotten worse." She said this bitterly. "He has no ability to stick when the going gets tough. It's Elizabeth's fault. She spoiled him."

She fell into a brooding silence and I found myself thinking that she was really more Geoffrey's sister than she was Bruce's. Bruce was a bit of an anomaly in the Cabot family. He was like none of the rest of them and probably Lynn was right in blaming Elizabeth for spoiling him. The behavioralists would like that explanation.

"There's something I don't understand," I said.

Immediately Lynn grew wary. "What's that?" Her voice sharpened.

"Bruce and Carole. What sort of crazy relationship do they have?"

She relaxed. What had she thought I was going to ask? I wondered.

"Just that," she replied, "a crazy relationship."

When she didn't elaborate I prodded gently. "I've heard rumors—and Bruce said something once—about Carole and Geoffrey."

Lynn chuckled mirthlessly. "Oh, yes," she scoffed, "the great Carole and Geoffrey rumor. You've seen Geoff. Do you for a minute believe there's anything in it?"

"As far as he's concerned, of course not. But how about Carole?"

Lynn shrugged expressively. "Who knows. Carole's a bit of a vamp. She'd like to have every attractive man within a hundred miles, and Geoff may not be charming but he's certainly a good-looking man. Carole's spoiled too. She did it first to spite Bruce. If Geoff had only given in to her, she probably would have thrown him away inside of a month. But her pride got hurt, so she keeps after him. Besides she knows that it drives Bruce wild. I think that's why she really does it. She cares about Bruce more than anyone. She won't give him up and she always comes back to him. There was the money, but—it's more than that. With Bruce too. They're birds of a feather." She stared past me, down the Box, and I felt that a dark, almost palpable curtain of despair had settled over her.

"Did Bruce have anything to do with Geoff's wife leaving?" I asked the question casually, hoping to catch her off guard. I wasn't even sure why I wanted to know, but somehow it seemed important.

She was cool again. "What makes you ask that?"

"Just curious."

"Curiosity or Sarah Gibson," she remarked sharply. "You'd do better than to listen to that woman's poison. I strongly suggest that you don't mention Nancy around here. Especially not to Geoff."

Her advice was well taken but a little late, I thought ruefully, remembering Geoff's anger. And then I realized that she had neatly side-stepped my question. They kept their secrets well, these Cabots.

"What was she like?"

"Nancy? She was a gentle, sweet, fragile girl. Impressionable. She wasn't capable of coping with us."

"And Geoff? Was he in love with her?"

Lynn gave me a funny smile. "He married her."

It wasn't what I'd asked. I began to wonder just what had happened between Geoffrey Cabot and his wife.

Lynn straightened suddenly, her supple, graceful body coming alive with movement. "It's late," she said, "and you're tired. How about a drink?"

It was around midnight. I couldn't sleep, so I slipped on my robe and went downstairs to the library intending to get something to read. Once in the library the liquor cabinet made me think of a drink. I fumbled through the cabinet until I found the gin and then searched a little more for the vermouth and ice. There was a fire burning. Even in the middle of summer, the Colorado nights were cool. I picked up my glass and moved over to a chair on the other side of the room. It was then that I noticed Geoff, slouched on the high-backed sofa.

"Mind if I join you?"

There were no lights in this half of the room and the flickering light of the fire cast shifting shadows on his face, making it even more unfathomable and forbidding. "Suit yourself," he answered gruffly.

We sat in silence. I sipped my drink and stared into the fire, uneasily aware of the tension in the room. The ceiling creaked occasionally as someone walked about upstairs. The fire sizzled quietly, devouring the logs, crumbling them into ashes. I tried to ignore Geoff and lose myself in contemplating the flames.

The martini was relaxing me and my mind was blank, concentrating only on the shapes of the fire, so I didn't see that Geoff had gotten up and come over to stand beside my chair until his arm swept into my line of vision. I heard the glass shatter against the fireplace and then realized what had happened. Startled, I looked up at him.

"Damn you, Jenny."

He looked exceptionally malevolent. It took all my control to ask calmly, "What's the matter, Geoff?"

He sneered at me and swept the glass out of my hand. It crashed against the mantel and I felt the cool wetness of the spilled gin on my legs. He grabbed me by the arms and jerked me out of the chair. I could feel his fingers biting cruelly into the flesh of my arms.

"Let go, Geoff," I snapped. "You're hurting me."

"I'll do a lot more than that. Do you realize that I could kill you right now? You could scream your head off and no one would ever hear, these old walls are so thick. You should be more careful, my dear Jenifer, if you're going to go about meddling in other people's affairs the way you do." Then the warning. "Get out of here. Get the hell out of our lives."

"If you're trying to make me afraid of you, you're succeeding admirably, but it's not going to stop me." My fear was suddenly forgotten; I was furious with him. "Why don't you admit it," I flared. "You're going to have to make an effort to be friends with your son, and you don't like it. You might have to give a little bit of yourself. That iceberg you've encased yourself in might have to melt." I could hear my voice whipping scornfully across the space between us. "Did you think it was going to be easy? That you could snap your fingers and Chris would come running to you? My God! You've got to be patient and gentle and try to understand him. But you can't do that, can you?" He still held me in his iron clasp, but I was oblivious to that now. The more I berated him, the angrier I had become. The words tumbled out, beating against one another like the water in a rapids, and I was heedless of what I was going to say until I had spoken.

"I said today that you used to take care of birds with broken wings, but you don't even do that anymore. You just pass them by. You don't care about a damn thing. I'm surprised you even aroused yourself to get angry with me. You cold-blooded bastard! No wonder your wife left you!" Too late I realized what I had said.

His hands tightened on my arms and his mouth twisted savagely. He pulled me even closer to him and his eyes were daggers, piercing through me. Before I realized what he meant to do, he bent his head toward me. I tried to turn away, but his hand was suddenly grasping my chin, holding it steady. His lips came down hard, brutally, upon mine.

I tried to shut off my mind, to endure his bitter, crushing kiss, but I was overwhelmed by a queasy, hollow feeling in the pit of my stomach. Then I was responding to him as I had refused to respond to Bruce.

He released me abruptly. "Bitch!" he ground out between clenched teeth as he shoved me down into the chair. He whirled and stalked out of the room.

I sat as I had landed, sprawled awkwardly across the chair. My lips were numb and I was shaking uncontrollably. Waves of nausea passed through me, but I stubbornly refused to give in to them. It was a long time before I could get up and go to bed.

CHAPTER 6

I was anything but rested when I finally got up the next morning. I had slept fitfully, plagued by dreams that were vague, but frightening, and that all seemed to contain the dark, angry figure of Geoffrey Cabot. He hovered over my nighttime imaginings like a bird of prey—like a rapacious hawk—ready to swoop and devour any vulnerable creature in his path. And I, I reminded myself, was all too vulnerable.

I felt as though I were inside a huge, multicolored, many-faceted globe that was spinning ever more rapidly, dizzying my mind with its kaleidoscope of colors and shapes, until I was sure of nothing, could trust nothing—not even my own judgments and intuitions. I knew that an easy solution wasn't available to me. I must try to pierce through the chamelion coats worn by the members of the Cabot household, trying to peer behind the masks they had donned. I must put on my own mask and dance time with the rest of them. And more than that, perhaps the hardest of all, I had to see through my own charade and discover just what it was I wanted here, what I was really trying to accomplish.

I stared at myself in the mirror above the big antique dresser. My eyes were dark, attesting to my lack of sleep. I took out my makeup kit and started to work on the dark circles. After about fifteen minutes, I stepped back to critically observe my handiwork. Not bad, I thought. Everyone will put it down to slight strain over Bruce. I thought about that for a moment. I knew I was avoiding dealing with my ambivalent feelings toward him. I would have to come to terms with them soon, but for today I was going to concentrate on other members of the Cabot family —one of whom was Geoffrey. I didn't like to admit how disturbing I found him.

The dining room was deserted. It was a little late for breakfast, so I went into the kitchen, found a lukewarm coffeepot and plugged it back in. More investigation led to the discovery of some English muffins. I tore one in half and slipped it into the toaster. Leaning against the cupboards, I looked around the kitchen. It was a good-sized room, with a huge bank of L-shaped cupboards and counters running along the wall at my back. They stopped against a double-oven stove at the end of the room. A round mahogany table filled the center of the room and high-backed, wrought-iron chairs stood around it. There was a fireplace at the other end. Nestled in the corner beside it was an old, comfortable looking sofa. A commode was along the wall opposite me, and a tall china closet was on the other side of the fireplace. It was a relaxing sort of room, quite different from the austere elegance of the dining room. A family room, I thought. It has a lived-in look and a quiet kind of dignity all of its own.

I sat down at the table, lit a cigarette and proceeded to try to sort out my plans for the day. I wanted to see Angus. I had a number of questions to which I needed answers. With a pang I thought of Christopher. I wasn't sure if Geoffrey would try to approach the boy again, or if he would cast him off even more violently than before.

I chewed thoughtfully on a crust from the muffin and frowned at my coffee cup. It was such a tangled morass, how could one person be expected to cope with it? It would have been enough just to deal with Bruce, but there were all the mysteries I had stumbled across as well. At first the reason I had come to Kingsville and the things that had been happening since I'd arrived had seemed separate puzzles. Now, as I thought of Geoff and Christopher, I found myself remembering the stipulation in my father's will. If I had been dead, he wanted everything to go to Geoff. Was it only because the land had originally belonged to Philip Cabot or was there something else? Was there a connection between my father's disappearance—murder if Sarah Gibson's hints were to be believed—and these attempts on Christopher? I had to find out.

I was still sitting, staring into my now empty coffee cup when Christopher opened the door and stepped into the kitchen. He sat down across from me, his arms resting on the table, and looked gravely at me.

"Hullo, Chris. I was just going to look for you. I didn't get a chance to talk to you last night. What did you do yesterday?"

He shrugged. "Aunt Lynn took me down to Paul's office and we moved stuff around."

I was unsure how to proceed. "Did something happen between you and your father last night?" I asked finally.

He looked puzzled for a moment. "*He* asked me what I'd done too. That was different I guess. He never does that. He hardly talks to me."

"Is that all?"

"He asked me a few more questions and then left." Again that quiet, reserved tone, his variant of his father's. I didn't wonder that Geoff had been frustrated. If only he'd have a little more patience. If only he really wanted to bridge the gap that separated him from his son.

"Christopher," I began firmly, "I know you're wary of your father and I know why. But I think you're mistaken." I said it with more conviction than I felt. I looked down at my hands for a moment and then plunged on. "I had a talk with him yesterday, and I told him that he should spend more time with you. I think if he got to know you things would be a lot better. That's what he was trying to do last night, only he doesn't really know how."

Christopher was alarmed. "No! You shouldn't have. I have to stay out of his way. If he doesn't notice me, then it's all right. He hates me." His voice broke on the last sentence.

"Nonsense," I told him stoutly. "You've got to be patient with him—help him." Why in God's name I was pleading Geoffrey Cabot's cause I didn't know, but it seemed that I was.

Christopher regarded me soberly, weighing the merits of my advice. He was a little adult, forced to grow up before his time.

Returning his gaze, I saw again how much he looked like his father.

Before he had a chance to answer me, the door swung open and Geoffrey strode into the room. I looked up at the sound of his footsteps and felt a cold wave of fear pass through me. I kept my face calm, determined that I was not going to be the one to bring up the scene between us the night before. Apparently, neither was he. In fact, he ignored me.

"Chris, I have to go up to the King and Queen today, and I thought maybe you'd like to ride up with me." It was a stilted invitation, but at least he had asked.

I held my breath, waiting for Christopher's answer. He considered his father for a while and then moved his head slightly to look across at me. "Okay," he announced. "I'll have to put my boots on. Will you wait?"

"Sure."

Chris slid out of the chair and ran from the room. I exhaled and hoped desperately that I was doing the right thing. Geoff looked at me then, gave me a long, cool glance and without a word, turned and left the kitchen.

I waited until I heard them leave, then I found Elizabeth and told her that I was going down to Kingsville and not to expect me for lunch. I ran upstairs, grabbed my sunglasses, a jacket and my car keys and stuffed my credit cards and some money in my jeans pockets. Seconds later I was in the car, turning the key in the ignition, feeling immensely relieved. I was glad to be out of the Castle.

———◆———

Angus wasn't at the hotel. A sign on the door read "Gone fishing." I smiled to myself. Apparently, I had been Angus' last boarder. I stopped at the cafe, asked where he usually went and received precise directions to his favorite stretch of the river. I found him with little trouble. He was standing in the middle of the river, playing a big trout. I waited until he had landed the fish and then hailed him. He looked up briefly, nodded, and then making sure the fish was safely in his creel, waded to the bank.

"Come down to go fishing?" he greeted me.

"No. I want to talk to you."

"Didn't know there was anything in Kingsville important enough to interrupt a man when he's fishing. They're biting good today. Salmon flies are up river this far. It's only once a year you catch it like this." He sat down on the river bank, took the fish he had just caught out of his creel and banged its head on a rock to kill it before he cleaned it. "What's on your mind, Jenny?"

I didn't know where to start. There were no beginnings or ends, only a mass of threads. I picked one. "I want to know about Geoffrey Cabot."

Angus' blade hesitated momentarily as he was slitting open the white-gray belly of the trout. "Geoffrey. You grew up with him. You should know as much as anybody."

"I trust you Angus. You've been around Kingsville a long time. I want to know what you think of him. What kind of man is he? How does he feel about his son?"

Angus pulled the intestines of the fish out and held them up for a moment and then threw them in the river. He finished cleaning the fish and put it back in his creel, pulling some grass by the bank and laying it in on top of the fish. Then he looked up at me, squinting against the sun, his grizzled face betraying nothing.

"Geoffrey Cabot. There's not much to say. He keeps to himself. No one reallys knows much about him. He's got no friends to speak of. He works for his uncle. Or his stepfather if you prefer to think of it that way. He's good at what he does, and King knows it. It's really Geoffrey that keeps Colvada Mining going. Too bad he'll never get anything out of it."

"But do you trust him?"

He shrugged. "Aye. As much as anybody I suppose."

"Do you think he's capable of violence?"

"Mebbe," Angus answered and then immediately added the qualifier. "But then we all are, aren't we. Human beings are a violent lot I think you'll find."

"How do you think he feels about Christopher?"

"What do you got in mind, Jenifer? You're asking a lot of questions."

I tried being reasonable. "Look, Angus. You've been tossing warnings at me ever since I got there. Something's wrong at the Castle you said. Well, you're right. If I'm going to deal with it, I need some information from you. What did you mean when you told me that?"

"Not much. I make it a habit of observing people. Like you said, I've been here a long time. Winters there's not much else to do up here. There's a lot of unhappy people around. Rumor has it that Bruce and Carole haven't been getting along so well. You had a bad time once. I just wanted you to be careful, that's all."

His explanation sounded reasonable enough, but I couldn't rid myself of the feeling that there was more to Angus' warnings than his superficial account covered.

"Yes," I said. "I heard the story that Carole and Geoffrey are playing around."

Angus snorted. "You been talking to Sarah Gibson. That's her pet rumor. She shore does hate the Cabots." He chuckled. He took his pipe out of his pocket and began filling it.

"Why?"

"Folks say it's because Elizabeth fired her for no good reason twenty-five years ago."

"Do you think it's true? About Geoff and Carole I mean?"

He drew on his pipe, sucking the flame of the match down into the bowl. "Well now," he said finally, "I don't suppose Carole would mind none. But Geoff . . ." He took the pipe out of his mouth and exhaled a long stream of smoke. "He keeps to himself. Everyone was real surprised when he married Nancy. She was a quiet, pretty thing, kind of fragile. I don't suppose Geoff come around much even for her. Bruce was always hanging around her though. All that and not liking the country—it's a wonder she stayed as long as she did, I guess."

"Why didn't she take Christopher with her?"

"He's a Cabot," Angus reminded me sharply.

"So. What's that got to do with it?"

He smiled at me sympathetically. "You should know that

without asking. He was then, and he still is, the only Cabot heir. That is, until Bruce and Carole have children. King and Elizabeth weren't going to let him go away. They made a handsome settlement on Nancy, but that was one of the conditions. The boy stayed."

"I see." I puzzled over what Angus had told me. It never occurred to me that Christopher would be the eventual Cabot heir. Was that the reason behind the attacks on him? If it was, then Geoff certainly had no motive. For some reason I felt absurdly pleased. Who then, I wondered. Bruce? Lynn?

"That all you had on your mind?" Angus asked.

His question reminded me that I had been focusing on the younger generation of Cabots. I needed to know about the older generation as well. "Tell me about Philip Cabot."

He looked at me closely as though he were sizing up my motives in asking. "Phil Cabot was a fine man. Not so serious as King, but then that come from being the younger brother. He knew he wouldn't have King's responsibilities. He always used to come down to the bar to play poker or pan with the boys. He liked to laugh and have a good time. He and Elizabeth made a handsome couple. She was a real looker when she was young. And Philip—he always was a good-looking devil. Dark. Just like Geoffrey."

"How much control of Colvada Mining did Philip have?"

"None. Same as Geoff. The Cabots don't believe in splitting the riches. It all goes to the oldest. They take care of everyone else of course."

"Then Philip owned nothing. No land, no mines, no claims?"

"You know something I don't?" He shot the question at me.

"Why, Angus," I reproved him. "How could that be?" I had to struggle to keep from smiling.

Angus tapped his pipe against a rock. "You're thinking about the land up Cottonwood, aren't you?"

I rubbed my tongue nervously against the inside of my cheek, wondering how on earth Angus had guessed that. "Maybe," I replied cautiously.

He smiled in remembrance. "It was Phil's all right. I remember when he bought it, oh, forty years ago at least. He tracked down some long-lost relative of old Dick McGuire's and bought it from her. He and your dad had this crazy obsession that there was ore up that gol-darned creek." Angus laughed. "Why everybody knows that there isn't even a salted mine up there. Damn fools. Both of them should have known better. Phil was a little touchy about it. I think he always hoped that he would make a strike that would overshadow anything King would ever do for Colvada Mining. He was sensitive about being the 'other one' of the Cabot sons. He was always trying to do something spectacular, but he was never serious enough about any of it. I don't know how your dad got ahold of it, or when for that matter. I don't suppose there's anybody around who could tell you except the two of them, and they're dead. Who knows, mebbe Phil just gave up on that Cottonwood idea and turned it over to your dad real quiet like so nobody would ever know how foolish he'd been."

It sounded plausible, but I was beginning to be wary of pat explanations. "Just exactly how did you know that my father had gotten hold of the land?"

"That Eastern fellow—Greenberg—that wants to buy it. He comes into the bar every now and then, and he was trying to pump me about you. Seems like everybody wants information these days," Angus finished significantly.

"Seems like you're one of the few people around here who knows anything," I told him pointedly.

He grinned at me, his eyes disappearing in a mass of wrinkles.

"Okay," I said quickly wanting to take advantage of his good mood, "let's go back to Philip. I'd like to know the terms of his will. It must be on file. It had to go through probate. Could you go to Telluride and look it up for me?"

Angus was busy cleaning his pipe. "In other words, you don't want anybody to know you're interested." It was a statement not a question.

"Mebbe," I mocked his laconic Western drawl.

His eyes crinkled in a smile. "I been watching people a long time. Gets so you know what they're going to do, what they're like. You've changed a lot." He nodded, satisfied, as if confirming his own statement. "You got more spunk now. That's good."

"I didn't ask you to analyze me, Angus. Will you do it?"

"I reckon so. I'll go over this afternoon. Don't have nothing better to do. Be too hot for the fish to bite by then." He placed one of his big, calloused hands over mine. "You're asking all the right questions, Jenifer. I haven't got any answers. I was sort of hoping you'd figure them out."

"Then how about telling me why you think there's something strange going on at the Castle."

"I've nothing much to go on. Just little things mostly. Lynn, for example."

"She's changed a great deal," I agreed. "Why?"

"Nobody knows. Not even Paul, I'd wager. Happened all of a sudden. About three years ago. Damn shame," he muttered. "She was a fine woman. Best of all the Cabots.

I nodded in agreement. "Anything else?"

"There's the boy."

"What about Christopher?" I cut in sharply.

"He's a pretty resourceful little fellow. He's had to be. Like Geoff in lots of ways. But he's friendly. He used to come down to see me, and I'd bring him fishing sometimes. Lately he hasn't been down much, and the last time I saw him he looked like he was afraid of something. I was worried about him. Other than that, I don't know. An old man gets to have intuitions, feelings about things. I've got bad feelings about that family. Mebbe it's just that wife of Bruce's. She can stir things up enough, God knows, but the rest of them too. Geoff and Lynn and Bruce." He shook his head. "It can't lead to anything good."

Characteristically, Angus was telling me something without telling me everything. I had to be sure what he meant. "Are you talking about violence?" I asked him bluntly. He looked shocked.

"Violence! Why no. I hadn't thought of it like that. No, I just meant bad blood between people. People using each other, not listening to each other. It always ends up with hurt and pain and lives getting twisted. Not to be unfeeling," he said gently, "but you should know. That's why I was hoping you could do something."

I sensed that Angus was telling me all he knew. He caught the feeling tone, but he didn't go far enough. He would be a useful ally, but I was going to be on my own as far as figuring out which of the inhabitants of Castle Cabot not only wanted to harm a nine-year-old boy, but which one was capable of it.

———◆———

I left Angus and went to see Paul. We drove to Cortez to meet with Dan Greenberg, the man who wanted to buy the Cottonwood property, so I didn't find out about the accident until late afternoon when I got back to the Castle. As I pulled into the driveway I saw that Elizabeth and Geoffrey were on the steps apparently arguing.

"Really, Elizabeth," I heard Geoff say, "why should I bother? You never did."

He turned abruptly, ran down the steps and vaulted into the jeep. Gravel spit out behind the tires as he drove rapidly away. I stared after him for a moment and then walked up to Elizabeth.

"I just don't know what to do with him," she said as I came up to her. "He's always been difficult. He rather frightens me sometimes."

I didn't know what to say. Elizabeth seldom talked of the way she felt about her family. Everyone knew that she disliked Geoffrey and doted on Bruce, but it wasn't because she ever talked about it. Within the clan the Cabots would quarrel, but to all outsiders they presented a united front. Elizabeth, I had always felt, was the architect of this solidarity.

She sighed. "All my children. I don't know what I did wrong. I spoiled Bruce. Lynn, the last few years, has gotten to be almost as impossible as Geoffrey. But enough," she smiled. "I've been wanting to talk to you, Jenny. Do you mind?"

"No, of course not," I assured her, wondering what was coming now.

"Why don't we go inside to the library. It's more comfortable."

I assented and followed her. No matter what, Elizabeth was always calm and gracious. She was dressed in yellow today, I noticed absently—a brightly flowered blouse and stylish bell-bottomed slacks. The tucked in blouse emphasized that she had kept a youthful figure.

"I know you're going to think that I'm prying," she began as she closed the door to the library, "and of course I am." She hesitated as though unsure how to proceed.

I had a hunch what she had in mind. "You want to know how I feel about Bruce?"

She seemed relieved that she hadn't had to ask me. "You're very perceptive, Jenny."

I considered what to tell her. "I don't think it matters how I feel," I said at last. "Bruce is committed to Carole and she's not about to give him up." It was the same answer I had given Lynn, and I hoped it would reassure Elizabeth that I wasn't out to cause trouble. At the same time, I had once again avoided resolving my ambivalence about Bruce.

"I appreciate your frankness." She paused, making a decision about what to say next. I leaned against one of the high-backed chairs. She made up her mind suddenly. "I hope you don't mind if I talk to you. I've been thinking about these things for a long time, and there has been no one to listen since John died. Your father was a very sympathetic man. I don't know if you realized that. And Kingston just humors me. You see, I'm a strong family person. I believe in having a family tradition and in having heirs to carry on. There's Christopher. Thank God for him. But Carole is not inclined to have children. I never was sure she was the right wife for Bruce, but he chose her and so I kept silent. I always liked you, Jenny, and when you came back so suddenly, I must admit that I half hoped you and Bruce would get back together. His hasn't been a happy marriage as I'm sure you've seen."

She was smiling at me, the gracious matriarch. I wondered suddenly if Bruce had put her up to talking to me, if he had gone to his mother as a way of circumventing Carole. I could see no other reason for Elizabeth's unprecedented confidences.

"It's been a long time," she was saying, "and you and Bruce have both changed, of course, but why don't you give it a chance. As you say, Carole will undoubtedly be difficult, but I think she can be handled if it is done properly."

With money, I thought cynically, certain that was what she had in mind. They would buy Carole off with the Cabot money, the way they had Geoff's wife. I was astounded by this turn of events. It was something I never would have expected, and I found it disconcerting. I had been shielding myself behind the hopelessness of the situation. Now I would have to face it squarely.

Before I could reply Kingston entered the room, slamming the door behind him. "Elizabeth!" I could hear the concern in his voice. "What's this I hear about Christopher?" he asked anxiously. Immediately, I was alert.

Elizabeth went over to meet him, giving him a kiss on the cheek. "He's all right. There's no cause to worry."

"What happened?" he demanded.

"Apparently he and Geoffrey were out riding and his horse bolted. He fell off. He has a broken arm, but he'll be fine."

"Is he in the hospital?"

"No. Lynn took him down to Don Mason, and Don set the break. He's upstairs. Lynn is with him."

"Where's Geoff?"

Elizabeth's lips drew tight at that. "I don't know. Does it matter?" Dislike sharpened her tone.

They stared at each other, both oblivious to my presence. Quietly, I slipped past them into the hall. Another "accident" I thought worriedly, and this time Christopher had been hurt. I wanted to see him.

I didn't get far. Bruce met me at the foot of the stairs and pulled me into King's office. He was his usual buoyant self.

"Jenny. Did Elizabeth talk to you?"

I looked at him uncomprehendingly. My mind was fixed on Christopher. Then I remembered what Elizabeth and I had been talking about. "Yes, she did."

"Good." He was beaming. "I've been frantic not being able to get you alone. I was afraid you'd misunderstand that whole business with Carole yesterday. While you were gone she kept badgering me and threatening. That was when I thought of Elizabeth, so I pretended to knuckle under to Carole to shut her up. With Elizabeth on our side, we don't have to worry. She can take care of Carole. She and King will pay her off, like they did Nancy. That's all Carole cares about anyway is the money. And as soon as we get married and have some kids, everything will be okay again." He was infectiously optimistic, like a little boy. Everything seemed so simple to him once he had thought of running to his mother.

I was uneasy. I didn't want to think about Bruce just now. I was concerned about Christopher. The attempts on his life were more important than the problem of what to do about Bruce. That could wait.

"Bruce," firmly I removed his arm from my shoulders. "It's not that simple. I'm not sure I want to marry you."

He looked at me in disbelief. "What do you mean?"

"There are too many things happening. I don't know what I want. I've got to have time to sort through them all."

"It's Geoff!" he burst out. "It's Geoff, isn't it? You're after him because of the money."

"I'm not after Geoff," I told him patiently, emphasizing each word hoping he would understand.

A peal of laughter from the doorway made us both whirl. Carole was lounging insolently against the door. She was clearly amused. I wondered how much she had overheard. "Well, well." She laughed again. "It seems you're stuck with me, Bruce dear. And you know King won't change his mind. We're penniless. Hangers-on at court." She dissolved into another peal of mirth.

Bruce glared at her. Once again I was the third party to a scene between two of the Cabots. I wanted none of this one either. I started to move toward the door.

"Jenny," Bruce pleaded. "You've got to marry me." I could hear the desperation in his voice, and I suddenly felt sorry for him. In a flash of understanding I saw him whole as I had never done before. He was a sad ghost of the eagle who had once flown across my sky.

"Don't press me, Bruce. Please. We'll talk about it later. Now, if you don't mind, I want to see Christopher."

I spent the rest of the day with Christopher. Lynn was there most of the time so I couldn't ask him what had happened. He was pale and withdrawn, reluctant to talk about anything. He and Lynn played checkers while I watched or chatted inanely about whatever came to mind. I knew that to have had an accident while riding with his father must have confirmed his deep-rooted fear that Geoff was trying to kill him; that he hated him. If Geoff would only break through that barrier. None of the rest of us could. Chris would only smile and nod and remain steadfast in his belief. And the worst part of it was, I told myself with a sinking heart, that I wasn't completely sure Christopher wasn't right.

Elizabeth brought Christopher's dinner on a tray. Lynn insisted on staying with him, sending me down to join the rest of the family. Afterward I went back upstairs. About an hour later the door opened and Geoff came in. He stood beside the bed, towering over it, the lamp behind him casting a long narrow shadow across the room.

"Hi, Chris," he greeted his son. "How does the arm feel?"

"Fine." Christopher might have been answering a problem posed in school.

"How long will you have that thing on?" He gestured toward the cast that covered Christopher's left forearm. "Did Don Mason say?"

The boy shook his head. "I have to see him next week."

Geoff flashed me an angry look as if to say that he was wasting his time and that it was my fault. I stared back, unwilling to admit to him how hopeless it all seemed. "When you get it off, we'll have to go riding again. You did well to hang on for as long as you did." He spoke awkwardly, clearly unused to praising his son.

Christopher caught his upper lip in his teeth and looked up at his father with that small, tight expression I had seen so many times. "I'm sorry I fell off. And I'm sorry if I was any bother to you."

I closed my eyes, feeling as though I wanted to cry. I looked at Lynn. Her head was down, staring at the checker board.

"Nonsense," I heard Geoff tell his son gruffly. "It wasn't your fault." When he received no reply Geoff looked at a loss. I knew how he felt. He decided to cut and run. "Well, I've work to do. Glad you're feeling okay. I'll look in on you again tonight or tomorrow morning." Christopher's grave blue eyes followed him as he left the room.

Without comment Christopher and Lynn resumed their game. I slipped out of the room wanting to catch Geoff. I needed to know his version of what had happened. And I had an idea about how he could break the ice with Christopher. I found him in King's office. He was about to pick up a sheaf of papers when I burst in. He grimaced as he saw me, but didn't say anything.

"Geoff," I began a bit breathlessly. "What happened?" I expected to have to coax him into telling me. Instead he answered immediately, still shuffling through the papers in his hand.

"We were in Rob Roy Basin, going to come down the escarpment. He'd gone on ahead of me a bit and his horse bolted. I cut down through the trees trying to head him off, but I didn't make it in time." He paused and looked at me then with that penetrating ice-blue gaze. "You were right, you know. It wasn't an accident. His saddle came off the horse. The cinch had been cut. It was a clever job. Whoever did it knew what they were doing. It was cut near where it's sewn onto the saddle. You never really look at that side of the saddle when you're cinching a horse up. The spot would be weakened every time the cinch is tightened until a sudden pressure would cause it to snap. I brought him down here and then went back up to get the saddle, but it was gone."

"Gone! but how?"

"I don't know. Of course nobody saw it but me, so you've just my word for it." His voice cut across the space between us, suddenly savage and bitter. "Maybe I made it all up."

I shrugged. "Why would you go to all that trouble?"

"To get you to trust me so that when I do succeed in killing him, it won't occur to you that I'll have to kill you too." His tone was malicious, taunting.

I winced. Behind his ugly jeering I thought I could detect anguish. Or maybe I merely wanted to. I made a movement with my hand. "Geoff. Don't."

"Why not?" he sneered. "That's what you think, isn't it?"

I bit my lip. He was right. I was tempted to think exactly that. I looked at him and although my voice was calm, my pulse was racing. "Look, Geoff, I'll be honest with you. I threw that at you yesterday because I was angry and I was trying desperately to find some way of getting through to you, of getting you to realize how frightened Christopher is and how much danger he's in. I don't know what to think about you. I guess I never have. You frighten me sometimes. But—" I shook my head— "if I really felt you were a murderer, I wouldn't have tried to get through to you about Chris in the first place."

He gave me a strange look, and when he spoke it was in his usual cool, detached tone. "You're a little fool, Jenny. But you've got guts, I'll say that for you."

"No, I haven't. It's just that sometimes there isn't anything else you can do."

"You could leave. There's nothing to stop you. None of this is really your affair."

"I can't. Not this time. If anything happens to that boy . . ." I left the sentence unfinished, a bit shaken by the way I felt. I hadn't realized until now how much Christopher meant to me.

"You've gotten very fond of Christopher, haven't you?"

"About Christopher," I said side-stepping his question.

"Look," he cut in impatiently throwing the papers on the desk. "I tried. You saw how he was. He hardly says two words. I can't do any more."

"You're a fine one to talk," I reprimanded him hotly. "If he hardly says anything, I wonder whom he gets it from. The burden of proof is on you, Geoff. You have to show him that you care." He stood there looking overly patient and sardonic. My determination flagged. "Oh, what the hell's the use!" I could hear the tired despair in my voice. I walked over to the bookcase and leaned my head against it. I couldn't bear to look at him any longer.

"You don't care about him. Why should I?" He had been right. I was a fool. An egotistic fool to think that I might straighten out the tangled mess the Cabots had made of their lives. A fool to think that anything about my father mattered. Let them take care of their own, if they could. It was no affair of mine.

Geoff's hand on my shoulder brought me out of my thoughts. "You're wrong, you know. I do care about him." He turned me to face him. His blue eyes were so intense that I couldn't meet his gaze. I felt my heart give a sudden jolt. "What do you think I should do?"

Geoff continued to bewilder me. "I think," I began stumblingly, "that Chris is going to have to be more careful about climbing around with that cast, and if you were to get him a dog —a puppy. He wants one, and it would be company for him. Maybe it would break the ice."

He considered the idea. "A dog, huh?" For the first time I saw him really smile. My pulse throbbed uncomfortably in my throat. "Okay, Jenny. I think I know where I can get a German shepherd pup. I'll go down in the morning. Now, how about letting me get some work done?" His admonishment was gentle.

———◆———

Geoff kept his word.

Again, I had slept badly and my tenseness was only heightened when I came downstairs and discovered that Lynn was nowhere in evidence. Determined that someone should be looking after Christopher, I spent the day with him. It was also a good way of avoiding Bruce. I needed time to assimilate his proposal, Elizabeth's assurance that Carole could be bought off and my sudden perception of Bruce's desperation. Once I would have jumped at the chance to marry him, no matter how rocky the road. Now I hesitated, and I wasn't quite sure why. There were too many things to deal with at Castle Cabot—Bruce, Christopher, Geoff, Lynn—and the puzzle that had brought me back. My father. I couldn't solve them all at once, so I concentrated on Christopher.

I said nothing to him about the dog, not wanting to get his hopes up. I was sure that Geoff had merely given in to placate me, to get me to leave him alone. Christopher was taciturn as usual. Gradually, as the day progressed, he started to talk more. I sensed that he really liked having someone to talk to even though he was shy, and I let him pick his own topics, not wanting to force him into conversation. When he began to speak of his mother, I encouraged him to go on, hoping that by voicing his feelings he would be able to cope with them better. Talk it out the psychologists say. I had never really tried it myself, and in Christopher I saw a chance to help someone from becoming what I had become. If I could show him that someone cared about him. If I could get him to trust me. I knew that the night he had come to my room had been a momentary lapse on his part, a fleeting lowering of his guard, and that he had chosen me as a safe person to come to. He had been frightened, worried, a spring wound tight ready to snap, and he had thrown himself upon me as the nearest refuge. I could have been a rock or a tree. Now I wanted to build upon that moment.

Somewhere a voice told me that I was merely setting both of us up for a fall. I would get him to care and then I would leave, betraying his trust and affection as all the adults in his world had. And I—I already cared for him far too much.

But reason, at least in my case, was a feeble opponent for the strong currents of emotion I felt, and none of my mental meanderings stopped me from trying to reach him. By the middle of the afternoon I felt that I was making headway. I had suggested a picnic lunch by Rob Roy Falls, and he eagerly assented. We had raided the kitchen and fixed an elaborate basket filled with sandwiches, coke and cookies. We laughed and chatted through the picnic.

Then, suddenly, his guard came back up. "You're going back to San Francisco soon, aren't you?" he asked abruptly. He was gazing up at me with his father's blue eyes.

"Yes," I answered slowly. "I don't know exactly when, but I will be going home in a week or so."

He considered this for a moment. He sat staring down the valley. Then, almost shyly, he said, "Jenny—" I held my breath wondering what was to come. He hesitated briefly, then with that incredible directness children have, he asked, "I don't suppose you could stay here with us, could you?"

It was starting already. Well, I thought, I had asked for it. Now I had to deal with it. "No, Chris. I'm sorry." I tried to be as gentle as possible. "I'm very fond of you, but my home, my job are in San Francisco."

"You could stay if you wanted, couldn't you?" he persisted.

"There's nothing for me to do here. I do need a job, you know." I knew I was avoiding his question and I felt guilty about it.

"Not if you sell your land. Grandpa King says it's worth a lot."

I found that piece of information interesting in itself, but I didn't have time to think about it now. Christopher was more important. I didn't know what to say to him. What he said was true. I could sell the land and stay in Kingsville if I wanted.

"Is it because of Uncle Bruce?"

I frowned. "No. Not really. I'm a person who needs to be doing something. I can't just sit around. Even if I sold the land and had enough money to live on for a while, there still wouldn't be anything for me to do. I wish I could stay, but it really is impossible."

He seemed to accept that. He picked up a cookie with his good hand and nibbled at it. "It's funny," he said in between bites. "You can't stay and Aunt Lynn can't leave."

I looked at him sharply. Out of the mouths of babes, I thought. Christopher might have more information than I gave him credit for. "What do you mean, Chris? Why can't Lynn leave?"

"I don't know. She just keeps telling Paul that she can't leave the Castle. And when he offers to come live in the Castle after they're married, she says no. Sometimes I just can't help overhearing them," he apologized for his eavesdropping. "I don't think she's very happy," he concluded seriously.

"Strange," I murmured under my breath. I was going to ask him a few more questions when I noticed his eyes grow large and he stiffened, gazing at something behind me. I heard the crunch of footsteps on the path.

Determined not to show I was startled, I turned slowly to find Geoff coming toward us, a squirming puppy in his arms. I glanced quickly at Christopher. His eyes were like saucers. I switched my gaze back to Geoff. He didn't look at me but turned his attention to his son. I was just as glad. I needed a moment to cope with the unexpected surge of emotion I felt.

"You two are hard to track down," Geoff said easily. "This little fella," he nodded toward the pup, "has been getting impatient." He put the pup on the ground. It was a German shepherd, about six weeks old I guessed. It sat, its head cocked to one side, as though listening with its postage-stamp ears to hear what else Goeff would say.

Geoff knelt down and nudged the pup toward Christopher. "Go on, fella. Check out your new master." The dog tottered over to Chris and began sniffing at the boy's hand. Chris reached out and tentatively scratched the dog's ears. Encouraged, the pup wagged his tail, bounced up in Chris' lap and began vigorously licking his face.

"You mean he's mine?" Chris asked excitedly. My eyes clouded with tears. He sounded like any normal boy—there was no trace of that wary, solemn tone.

"That's right," Geoff assured him. "I thought it was about time you had a dog." He flicked his eyes at me. "He's a fine one too. Best of the litter. Of course, you'll have to take care of him. He's your responsibility."

Christopher's eyes shone. "Can he sleep in my room at night?"

A brief smile played over Geoff's lips. "Once he's house broken, I don't see why not."

Christopher fondled the pup for a moment and then, with a

little rush, he flung himself at Geoff. I could barely hear his choked thank you, muffled as it was against Geoff's shoulder. Geoff was startled, but after a moment he put his arms around him and the two dark heads closed together.

Sentimentalist that I was, I had a lump in my throat as I turned away and walked over to the falls.

CHAPTER 7

Lynn didn't appear until after dinner. Elizabeth seemed slightly annoyed that she was absent but said nothing. Kingston, from all outward appearances, was preoccupied and didn't really notice. Christopher was clearly feeling better. He didn't say much, but several times I caught him glancing shyly at Geoff. Geoff, for his part, remained calm and imperturbable. Dinner was a quiet enough affair. Bruce was glumly silent while Carole, apparently satisfied for the moment, refrained from her usual biting comments. We all settled into a routine of either ignoring each other or engaging in polite conversation.

Everyone dispersed after dinner. I half-expected Bruce to seek me out, but he didn't. I was, I realized, relieved. I went upstairs with Christopher, and chatted with him as he played with Strider, as he had promptly named his puppy. The family had taken the addition of the dog with their usual aplomb, although I could tell that King, in particular, was both surprised and pleased when Christopher told him that Geoff had given him the dog.

Later, I came back downstairs, thinking that I would take a walk. I heard voices raised in the foyer and paused on the landing uncertain about what to do. Recognizing Lynn's voice, I decided to listen in.

Her tone was laced with contempt. I wished I had caught the first part of the conversation. "You won't have to expect Paul anymore," she was saying.

There was a pause and then Elizabeth spoke. "So he's finally done it. I'm astounded that he put up with you for so long. You've handled it very badly, Lynn."

Lynn laughed shortly. It was an ugly laugh. "You'd have saved us all a lot of trouble, Elizabeth, if you didn't hate Geoff so much."

The door slammed and I waited for a while before I went down. I guessed that Lynn had gone out again and, on impulse, I decided to try to find her. From the sounds of things, she and Paul had broken up. Perhaps she would feel like talking. Following a hunch, I walked rapidly down the path which ran toward Mithral Falls. Lynn was there, sitting on the ground, her head in her hands.

"Lynn," I greeted her, trying to sound surprised. "Is something wrong?" I feigned ignorance.

Slowly she looked up. Her face was a mask of pain, bitterness and despair. She didn't say anything, just looked at me for a moment and then dropped her head. Thinking that directness was perhaps my best weapon, I attacked frontally. "You've quarreled with Paul." I made it a statement rather than a question.

Her head jerked up. "What makes you say that?" she snapped.

I pointed to her left hand. "You're not wearing your ring."

Involuntarily she glanced down at her shapely, tanned hand. There was a band of white skin on her third finger. "You're very observant," she told me dryly.

"Would you like to talk about it?"

She softened momentarily. "You're very kind, Jenny. I appreciate your concern, but there's nothing you can do." Then her face set in hard, battle lines. "It's no good, any of it. I've been unfair enough to Paul, keeping him hanging for so long. He deserves better than that, and I can't give it to him." Her voice was flat and forced, as though it cost more effort than she had to say the words.

"It's Christopher, isn't it? You have to stay here to watch him, follow him, to make sure that he doesn't get hurt."

"Christopher needs someone to fulfill a mother role, yes." Lynn agreed, deliberately misunderstanding me.

"That's not what I meant and you know it. You have to see

that whoever is trying to kill the boy won't succeed. Maybe you even know who it is," I challenged.

"Leave it alone, Jenny." She was angry. "It's not your concern. You'll only end up getting hurt."

If I had any doubts left about what was going on at Castle Cabot, her reply blotted them out. "Is it Geoff?" I asked fearfully, brushing aside her warning.

She gave me a piercing look and then replied evasively. "You shouldn't trust anyone, Jenny. You're playing with fire. Sell your father's land and get out. Go back to San Francisco and leave us to play our tawdry little games."

I shook my head. "I can't do that."

"Then you're more of a fool than I thought you were."

"I suppose I am," I agreed readily. I moved from the rock I had been leaning against and, walking over to Lynn, I knelt in front of her. I put my hand on her knee. "Lynn, trust me. Let me help."

The lashes swept down, covering her somber brown eyes, and she shook her head violently. "No. You're like Paul. Let us be, Jenny. There's nothing that can be done."

"Why don't you tell me," I suggested. When she shook her head in refusal I added, "I'll find out anyway."

"For your sake, I hope not."

Neither of us spoke for a long time, Lynn lost in her misery, I in my puzzles. Lynn's refusal to leave the Castle was tied up with Christopher. She must know who was behind the attacks on him. Again, I was faced with the question of who would want to harm the boy. Even if he were the eventual Cabot heir, that was still no reason for anyone to kill him. Suddenly Carole's voice replayed itself in my memory. She had taunted Bruce with King's refusal to change his mind. We're penniless, she'd said. And just before that Bruce had accused me of being after Geoff for the money. In my concern over Christopher, I'd paid no attention to the implications of their statements. Now I began to wonder if King had changed his will in favor of Geoff, or possibly in favor of Christopher with Geoff acting as the trustee for the estate. In either case, it gave Bruce an excellent motive.

"When did King change his will?" I slipped the question in casually, trying to catch Lynn off guard.

As I'd hoped, she replied automatically. "Five months—" She broke off and stared hard at me, her face a stony, impenetrable mask. There was a spark in her eyes that trembled beneath their impassive brown surface. She stood up. "I've underestimated you, Jenny. You're a fool, but you're clever. Maybe too much so for your own good." She turned abruptly and walked away.

With mixed feelings I watched her go back toward the Castle. I had no doubts now. Someone at Castle Cabot—most probably Bruce—was a killer. The stakes were high. The Cabot fortune, although affected by the economic uncertainty of metals, was considerable. Still, I paused in my headlong rush to conclusions. Something didn't quite fit. Why, I wondered, had King cut Bruce out, and exactly what were the terms of the new will? I sat in the deepening twilight with the mist from Mithral Falls drifting over me, and tried to sort through everything once more.

Lynn's broken-off reply convinced me that my guess had been correct. King's will had been changed five months ago. The attacks on Christopher must have begun shortly afterward. That would fit with Angus' observation that in the past few months Christopher had stopped coming to visit him. That meant either Christopher was the new heir or that Geoff had been made the heir because Christopher was the only grandchild.

Yet for years Lynn had refused to marry Paul or leave the Castle. She had changed suddenly, three or four years ago, Angus had said. She must have started her vigil then. But who was she watching? Bruce? It didn't make sense. And why? What had happened three years ago?

"Jesus!" I sat bolt upright and swore softly to myself. The two puzzles—my father and the Cabots—were back together again, overlaying each other, separated by the span of years. I had momentarily forgotten about the errand I had asked Angus to do. I would have to see him first thing in the morning.

———◆———

Angus was behind the bar, washing glasses. I slid onto a bar stool, cursing them for being so uncomfortable and leaned my elbows on the bar. "Mawning, Angus," I drawled in an exaggerated tone.

He didn't seem surprised to see me. "Howdy, Jenny," he greeted me. "Thought you'd be down yesterday. How's Christopher?"

"Fine."

"I suppose it was you that talked Geoff into getting him that pup. Damn fine thing, I say. You're doing a good job, Jenny. I knew you could."

I went straight to the point. I was in no mood to chat with Angus this morning. "Did you get to the courthouse to look at Philip Cabot's will?"

He had finished washing the glasses and now took up a towel and began to dry them. "Yep," he told me squinting his eyes as he held a glass up for inspection. "It's a regular sort of will. Drawn up by lawyers and all. He didn't have much. What he had, he left to Geoff with Elizabeth being the executor until Geoff was of age. There's no mention of the Cottonwood land."

Somehow I hadn't thought there would be. There was something strange about the way my father had gotten Philip Cabot's land. Then three years ago, father had disappeared. At the same time Lynn began to change. There had to be a connection.

"Tell me, Angus, did you ever think there was anything strange about my father's disappearance?"

"Strange?" he echoed. "What are you driving at, Jenny?"

"Sarah Gibson hinted he might have been murdered."

He snorted loudly. "Sarah! She's got a powerful good imagination. Reads too many of them Zane Grey books."

"So you think he just got lost, the way they say?"

"Never really thought about it one way or the other."

"But now that you think about it?"

"Doesn't matter how long a man's been in these mountains. Accidents happen. What do you got in mind, anyhow?"

I was tired of the secrecy, so I told him. I needed to bounce my suspicions off someone. "I think," I said slowly, feeling the full weight of my words, "that one of the Cabots killed my father."

Angus dropped the glass he was polishing. It shattered unheeded on the floor. I could see him chewing on the stem of his pipe. "That's pretty strong stuff. Why would anyone do a thing like that?"

"I'm not sure. The logical one is Geoff because of the land. I was hoping you'd be able to help me figure it out."

"John was a quiet man. I don't suppose anyone ever knew him real well. Kingston trusted him absolutely. So did Geoff as far as I could ever tell. I think you're letting Sarah Gibson put ideas in your head, Jenny."

I didn't agree, but I acquiesced for the moment. Where did I go from here? I wondered, drumming my fingers on the bar.

"By the way," Angus said, "a fellow named Alex Grainger called. Thought you were staying here. He said you should call him."

I frowned. Alex Grainger. What could he want? Asking Angus if I could use his phone, I got the operator and gave her the Cortez number. Alex Grainger answered. "Miss Trent," he said, "you know I've been thinking about your father since you were here the other day and I remembered that the last time I saw him he kept talking about some kind of stair. That's what made me think he'd gone off. I couldn't make any sense out of it. Maybe you can."

"A stair?" I repeated blankly. Then I remembered the scrap of paper I had found in the lockbox and had promptly forgotten. "Was it the Mithral Stair?" I asked.

His voice brightened. "Yes, that was it. Does it mean anything to you?"

It didn't yet, but I hoped it would. I thanked him for bothering to call me and went back to Angus.

"Angus, what's the Mithral Stair and where is it?" I held my breath hoping that he would know the answer.

He swung around to face me and a frown crossed his forehead. "The Mithral Stair! Why I haven't heard it mentioned in years. Had no idea anyone still used the name."

"But what is it?"

He stroked his beard and I could see him wondering why I wanted to know. "About fifty years ago—more or less—the escarpment was honeycombed with tunnels. Then the second Kingston Cabot decided to drive raises in each tunnel so that they'd all connect with each other, like a huge ladder you might say. He did it too, although no one could ever really see why. Just a whim. But then the Cabots are rich enough to give into foolish whims like that. When he was done you could go through the escarpment and come out by Mithral Falls. Eventually they drove tunnels the other way, too, so that you could get to the top of Rob Roy on the Stair.

"Now, Philip, when he was young, came up with the idea of calling the whole thing the Mithral Stair after Mithral Mountain since that's the geographic name for the escarpment. Instead of keeping the original names of the tunnels, he called each one a level. Said it was more like hell that way. He was a real deviler, that Philip." Angus smiled in remembrance.

Here was more than I had hoped for. With racing pulse, I asked my next question. "How many people know about this nickname of Philip's?"

Angus shrugged. "It was a family thing mostly. Everyone at that time knew of the name, but only the family used it."

I was getting excited now, more sure than ever of the connection between Father and whatever was going on now with the Cabots. I remembered the rest of the cryptic note. "Was the Grubstake one of the tunnels on the Stair?"

Angus nodded.

"Was it the fifth level?" I fired the question at him, like a staccato burst from a sten gun.

"I don't remember," he said slowly. "Could have been."

I began pacing rapidly in front of the bar. "So that's it," I said aloud although I was speaking more to myself than to Angus. "But why would it be so important?" Once again I had turned a corner only to find myself at a dead end. "It meant something to my father," I told Angus. "I found a note he'd left with the words, 'Mithral Stair, fifth level, hanging wall, Grubstake and

Flying Dutchman' on it. Do you have any idea what it might mean?"

"Well," he picked up his pipe from the bar and began scraping out the bowl. "The Grubstake was where Phil Cabot's accident happened. As for the Flying Dutchman—" He had dropped the comment casually, as though he were announcing that it might rain.

I whirled to face him. "What exactly *did* happen to Philip Cabot?" I demanded tensely.

"Mine accident," he drawled in his laconic mountainese. "One of those freak things that happens every once in a while. The hanging wall in the Grubstake was full of bad fractured rock. Phil liked to use the Stair to get up into Rob Roy. It was a Sunday, as I remember, so no one was working. Phil went up the Stair. They were going to blast the wall the next day and had begun to drill the holes. There was an explosion. The whole damn side and ceiling of the tunnel come in. Brought down the tunnel above it too. Phil was buried under it. We never did figure out how it happened. Geoffrey was with him. He was about five, I guess. He'd stopped to play and was just out of the range of the cave in. Fortunately, Phil had given him a hard hat and light so he was able to come back out the tunnel and told everyone what had happened."

The hanging wall, I thought. Things were starting to come together a little more. I started to wonder just how much of an accident Philip Cabot's death had been. And Geoff had been there. It must have made an indelible impression on a five-year-old boy's emotions. Did Elizabeth somehow blame Geoff for her first husband's death? Was that why she disliked him so? And if Philip Cabot's "accident" had been arranged, my father could well have had something to do with it. Here was another turn of events I hadn't expected. Father could have rigged the accident in order to get the Cottonwood land, or perhaps because he had already gotten it and Philip had found out.

"Elizabeth took it real hard," Angus was saying. "King always had been in love with her. The whole damn Box was. Anyway, they got married about nine months later and, of course, your mother married John."

I frowned. "What do you mean, 'of course'?"

"You never knew then? I always wondered. Your mother was getting fixed to marry King until the accident. He broke it off once Elizabeth was free, so she married John instead. He shore did love that woman," Angus wagged his head for emphasis. "The only two things I ever knew John to get excited about were mining and your mother. Damn near killed him when she died."

I stared blankly at Angus hardly believing what he had just told me. My mother and King Cabot! That gave my father an even greater incentive to put Philip out of the picture. Would there never be an end to the internecine relations? I pulled out a bar stool and sat down.

"I know it's before noon, Angus, but mix me a martini. I'll pay you when it's legal." He started to say something, then stopped himself. He bent down and pulled a bottle of gin from under the bar. I lit a cigarette and began, for what seemed like the hundredth time, to piece things together once again.

There had been two murders, it appeared, and the current attacks on Christopher. Bruce had the motive for trying to harm Chris, but he had no reason I could think of for murdering my father. Geoff, on the other hand, seemed to have a number of things to hold against my father—the land and, if my suspicions were correct, Philip Cabot's death. But why would Geoff want his son dead? None of it made sense, and I could think of no other likely suspects. Lynn didn't stand to profit from the will one way or the other, and she had nothing against my father. Both Elizabeth and King might have had reason for causing my father's disappearance, but no reason to move against Christopher. They were both fond of the boy. It was a jumbled mass of dead ends, truncated alleys, pieces that fit on one side of the puzzle but not on the other three.

My mind drifted back to the Mithral Stair. The Stair was intriguing. Only the Cabots would have done something so extravagant and whimsical. Since everything began there, perhaps if I dropped broad hints about being interested in it or even tried to find some of the tunnel maps, I could smoke out the killer. They would try for me instead of Christopher.

"Angus," I asked suddenly, "how can I get onto the Stair?"

"It's all sealed off. Has been since Phil died. The timbers are all rotted by now. You'd be signing your death warrant to go in there. After the accident King never had the heart to dig the body out. He left him in there and shut it up as a tomb. The escarpment was about played out anyway, and King shifted the mining operations to Red Canyon. No one's been on the Mithral Stair for thirty years."

I left Angus and drove down to see Sarah Gibson. She had been working for the Cabots when Philip's accident had happened. Maybe, I thought, I could get some useful information from her. Besides, I needed to talk to her about the furniture.

Her shop was closed when I drove up. She was in the back, vigorously wielding an ax. I watched for a moment as she split a log into two neat pieces. She definitely knew what she was about. I glanced around, noting how clean the place was.

She looked up as I approached her. "Oh, it's you again." She knocked the two pieces of wood off the chopping block and rested the ax on it, leaning on the handle. "Always like to get my wood cut in the summer," she explained. "Plan ahead, Ezra always said. Burn lots in the winter. Keeps the electricity bill down. You come to talk about your furniture I suppose."

We haggled over the quality of the pieces and the prices she would pay. She was, I discovered, a shrewd businesswoman. When we had finished I asked casually, "By the way, you knew Philip Cabot, didn't you?"

"Yes, I knew him." Her reply was uncharacteristically terse.

"What was he like?" I prodded.

For a while I thought she wasn't going to answer. Then, in an acid tone I hadn't heard her use before, she told me, "Philip was different from his brother. He wasn't so impressed with who he was as Kingston. Maybe that's because he wasn't nobody. He was gay. Fun loving, I guess you'd call it. They used to have big parties when Elizabeth first come. Geoffrey's not a bit like his father. He was allus a queer boy. Sullen. Quiet. I hoped that meant he had more sense than the rest of 'em, but he didn't. Married that mouse of a thing who fell for Bruce first chance she got and then run off. Them Cabots," she finished disgustedly. "Wouldn't give you two cents for any of 'em."

It was a curious, rambling answer to my question. "What made Elizabeth dislike Geoff so?"

She shrugged as if to say that it made no difference to her what the Cabots thought or felt. "No reason," she said shortly.

"But she must have a reason," I insisted. "It's so totally out of character."

"People don't need reasons." For the first time Sarah was uncommunicative.

"You were working for the Cabots when Philip was killed, weren't you?"

Immediately she was on the defensive. "Yes," she said shortly. "What about it?"

"What happened exactly?"

She didn't answer for a while, but leaned against the ax handle, her lined, flabby face thoughtful. I knew she was trying to figure out why I would want to know about something that had happened so long ago. I stared back at her.

"It was a mine accident. Damn shame too. He never had a chance."

"There's no question that it was an accident?"

" 'Course not," she snorted in surprise. "What else would it be? What's all that old history to you?" she asked suspiciously, her eyes narrowing as she looked at me.

"Just curious, that's all," I assured her blandly.

"Curiosity killed the cat," she said sharply, swinging the ax so that the head sunk into the chopping block, almost as though emphasizing her words. I felt a chill pass through me. Her comment could be simply one of a gossipy old small-town woman. On the other hand, it could be a veiled warning.

"So it did," I murmured.

She gave me a look which indicated that I had wasted her time, bent down to pick up a huge chunk of wood and heaved it onto the block. The sagging flesh on her upper arms tensed and tightened as she lifted the log, revealing what a strong woman she was.

"If you know what's good for you," she said pulling the ax out of the block, "you'll get out of that house and move back down with Angus. Old fool that he is, he's a lot better than them Cabots. If I hadn't liked your father so well, I wouldn't do business with you."

I left her then. Sarah Gibson had given me very little information, but she had greatly increased my sense of foreboding.

My next stop was at Paul Darcey's office. His battered car was parked outside so I knew he would be in. The outer office was empty. Walking through it, I knocked on the door to his office and heard him bid me to come in. I stopped short as I opened the door. Paul was leaning back in his red-leather swivel chair, his feet on his desk. The room was in its usual disheveled state. A quick glance told me that Paul looked terrible. His hair was more tousled than normal. There were bags under his eyes and a dark shadow of beard on his face. He looked at me expectantly, and I knew he was hoping that I was Lynn. I could see the disappointment cross his face. When he spoke, it was an effort.

"Hi, Jenny. Excuse the mess," he waved his hand at his office. "What can I do for you?" His voice was tired and lifeless.

"Maybe it's more a case of what I can do for you."

He moved his head slowly. "I don't understand what you mean."

I walked into the room, moved a pile of papers from a chair and sat down. Resting my elbows on the arms of the chair, I locked my fingers together and looked speculatively at Paul. I hadn't known exactly what I was going to say to him. "I talked with Lynn last night," I began. "What happened between the two of you?"

He made an aimless, bewildered gesture. "I guess I ran out of patience. I told her that I wanted to get married now. I was tired of being put off. She asked if that was an ultimatum, and when I said yes she told me she was calling the whole thing off. Said she's not ready to get married yet. Four years," he exploded, "and she's not ready yet."

I decided to tell him part of the story. "I'm going to be very frank with you, Paul. I know what's holding Lynn back. Something is very wrong at the Castle. It has been for years. The immediate danger is to Christopher. Ever since Kingston changed the will, someone has been trying to kill the boy."

Paul's emotional strain had dulled his normally sharp reactions. He stared at me in disbelief. "You're crazy," he croaked finally.

"I'm afraid not. I wish I were. I don't know who's behind it all. Lynn does—I'm sure of it. She's never told you because it's someone she's trying to protect. And whoever it is, she's been watching them for years, waiting for something like this to happen. That's why she could never marry you. She had to be up there. Watching. And she could never let you move into the Castle either, because she couldn't risk having you find out who it is."

Paul blinked several times in rapid succession as he struggled to digest what I'd told him. Then he was galvanized into action. His feet hit the floor with a crack and I heard the springs of the swivel chair contracting. He leaned forward, suddenly the lawyer again. "My God, Jenny! Do you realize what you're saying?" His voice rose in astonishment.

"Yes. I do."

"I don't believe it."

"You'd better. Like it or not, that's what's happening. King *did* change the will, didn't he?"

"Yes." He said it slowly, dragging the word into two syllables. "How did you find out about it?"

"Something Bruce and Carole said, and then I guessed the rest. Is Geoff the heir?" I wanted Paul to confirm my assumptions.

"That's privileged information you know."

I stared at him. I was sure of myself now, acting with the calm efficiency I had painstakingly cultivated over the years. "I realize that, but Christopher's life is at stake."

I fell silent, waiting for Paul to make his decision. He rubbed his hand absently across the stubble on his chin. "All right, Jenny," he said at last. "The Cabot estate is left in a trust for Christopher to be administered by Geoff. Geoff also receives a substantial sum of money. The rest of them are provided with annual incomes."

I nodded. "Why did King do it?"

"He never told me. Lynn says it's like a knight's gambit to force Bruce and Carole to have children."

I considered that. It explained the attacks on Christopher. The killer must be gambling that with Christopher out of the way, King wouldn't put Geoff ahead of his own son.

"What makes you so sure that you're right about all this?" Paul asked.

"That boulder that almost caught us on the talus the other day didn't fall by itself. I found fresh horse tracks and crowbar marks at the top of the cliff. Besides, Lynn's more or less confirmed my suspicions by warning me bluntly to mind my own business."

Paul shook his head several times. "I just can't believe it. If it is true, why are you telling me?"

"First, because I'm an incurable sentimentalist. Lynn loves you. The two of you should be together. Second, I need your help. Somehow my father got the Cottonwood property from Philip Cabot. I don't know how. You have access to the Cabot papers. I want you to try to find out for me. Also, there's that Cabot stock of my father's. I'd like to know when he got it and how. Then there was apparently a series of tunnels in the escarpment called the Mithral Stair. See if you can find a map of it for me. Quietly. I don't want either King or Geoff to know you're looking for it. And don't mention any of this talk to Lynn. As I said, she's warned me off already."

He got up and paced around the room, nervously running his hand through his hair, alternately smoothing and then rumpling it. I reached over, ruffled through some papers, found a cigarette on his desk, lit it and sat back to watch him. I was waiting for him to ask me what my father and the Cottonwood property had to do with the threat to Christopher's life. He stopped finally and came over to sit on the corner of the desk facing me. "How did you get into all this?"

I shrugged. "I don't know really. It just happened. My father I suppose. I got curious." I smiled at him disarmingly.

"What does your father have to do with it?" he queried, his bloodshot eyes watching me intently.

I pondered about what to tell him. I trusted Paul, but I didn't know enough yet. I evaded the question. "Let's just say I don't think he disappeared, and I don't think Lynn does either."

Paul's lips were drawn in a thin, bloodless line, his face was haggard. He stared past me. Inadvertently, I sighed softly. There was a canker in the lifeblood of the Cabots, twisting them into grotesque shapes, tainting everyone who touched them. Paul should have been happy, gay, carefree and instead he was grim, solemn, miserable. Lynn, who was once soft and gentle and refreshingly open, had turned into a hard, bitterly cautious, closed-off woman. While I . . .

I cut off my thoughts. "You'll see Lynn?" I asked him.

"You're so very sure that's what she wants?"

I considered his question. How could anyone really know what another person wanted? It would be what I would want if I were in Lynn's position, or what I thought was Lynn's position, I modified. I met his gaze steadily. "I think it's not only what Lynn really wants, but what she needs. Don't give up now, Paul."

He was silent for a long while. Then he nodded and spoke with deliberation. "I don't know quite what to make of you or your story, Jenny, but I'll go along with you for a while. I just hope you know what you're talking about."

"Good," I told him heartily. I stood up, vigorously confident. "Hopefully, we'll clear all this up soon. And Paul," I added as I walked to the door, "get some sleep." I smiled at him fondly. My initial liking for him had grown considerably.

◆

I stopped at the mill office and got a map of Rob Roy Basin from Geoff. I made a point of telling him I wanted to explore the old tunnel adits in the Basin for relics. I left the car at the Castle and made the same announcement to Lynn adding that I had just heard about the Mithral Stair and was intrigued to see which tunnels in the Basin had led to it. Then I began the arduous climb up the jeep road which had been carved out of the Kingsville escarpment.

I knew that by dropping hints about the Stair I was taking a desperate, daring gamble, but it was the only chance I had. Maybe, I thought, if I get close enough to the truth, I could force Lynn into revealing what she knew. Only then would the cycle of violence that had engulfed the Cabot family stop.

It took almost an hour to walk to the top of Rob Roy Falls. I was winded and perspiring when, at last, I arrived. I waded into the stream, letting the cold water seep into my tennis shoes, soothing my aching feet, while I surveyed the Basin. It was the north side of the long narrow Basin that I was interested in. I could see old mine dumps at various intervals. Moving out of the stream, my feet quite cold now, I sat down on the grass to let my sneakers dry in the sun. Once again, as I had the first day I had been back in Kingsville, I looked toward the massive ruins of the Rob Roy Mine and then my gaze settled on the old tramway stop with its warning sign. Dangerous. Keep out. Private. The words didn't just apply to abandoned buildings, I thought, they characterized the entire Cabot family.

Determinedly I set about my self-appointed search. It took me the better part of another hour to walk halfway up the Basin. Then, using the map I had gotten from Geoff, I carefully came back toward the Falls, inspecting each tunnel adit as I passed. The map gave them names—The Little Nellie, The Birdie, The Leadore, Silverhill, The Whitestone, The Duchess. They were all the same. Twisted grotesque pieces of track lay on the mine dumps along with an occasional dark brown mine car, which had usually been there so long that the metal was paper thin, even pocked with holes, as though it had been attacked by an army of minute moths. The tunnel entrances were choked with rock, and I wondered if they had been dynamited shut. I was certain that all of them had led, in some circuitous way or other, onto the Mithral Stair.

It was late afternoon when I got back to the top of the Falls. I rested for a while, bathing my face with the cool water from the stream. Then I wandered over to stand near the brink of the Falls. The creek rushed, bubbling and churning, over the precipice. Relaxing in the sun, I let myself be mesmerized for a moment by the quickly flowing water.

I didn't hear the noise until it was too late. It took me a moment to collect myself, and then I began to turn slowly so that all I saw was a shapeless figure, its face completely covered by the kind of pullover masks bank robbers wear, and the dark, gloved hands that reached out to push me over the Falls.

I jerked violently to the side, the hands shoving against my shoulder instead of my back as the killer had intended, and I stumbled as I tried to get out of the way. My ankle twisted and I saw the ground coming up to meet me, and then, blissfully, I knew nothing more.

———◆———

I opened my eyes slowly. All I could see was a blue blur and I wondered if I was still alive. A movement of my head that resulted in a sharp, stabbing pain reassured me. Something wet and sticky crept down my cheek. Gingerly, I raised my hand to wipe it away and realized that it was blood. I fought down a wave of nausea. Again I tried moving my head and again the pain shot across it, making a red diffused blur in front of my eyes. I groaned.

"Take it easy." The voice came from somewhere to my left. A figure drifted above me. I blinked, trying to clear the hazy double image.

It was Geoff.

He knelt beside me and put his hand under my head to steady it, while he gently dabbed at my forehead with a cool, damp cloth. Unprotestingly, I closed my eyes and let him continue. After a while he spoke again. "How do you feel now?"

"Lousy," I answered succinctly, surprised that my voice was as steady and strong as it sounded.

"Here," he said, "hold this." He placed my hand on the wet cloth that was draped across my forehead. "Think you can try to sit up?" He was brusque, businesslike.

I took the cloth away from my head and started to push myself up. The sharp pain had subsided and given way to a dull throbbing. I drew my brows together in an effort to control the ache, and quickly Geoff put his arm behind me and helped me into a sitting position. Feeling as though a hundred Hottentots were doing a hammer dance inside my skull, I was grateful for his support.

I found the cloth and started to press it to my forehead where I could feel the blood again beginning to flow. Geoff sat down, slightly behind me, bracing my weight against his body. Without saying anything he took the cloth from me and turning my head toward him, pressed it firmly against the gash. Meekly, I leaned against his shoulder. His hands were quick and sure as though he'd done this many times. His gaze was cool and impersonal.

He had gotten here very quickly, I thought. Maybe he had been the formless, masked figure who had been so intent on pushing me over the Falls. I had no idea how long I'd been unconscious.

It became important that I know. It had been close to five-thirty when I'd gotten back to the Falls. I turned my wrist and managed to glance at my watch. The figures on the dial were a bit fuzzy but I could tell that it was nearly six. Almost half an hour. I wondered how long Geoff had been bending over me and why, if he were the killer, he hadn't just thrown me over the Falls. No, I decided, it couldn't be Geoff. But then how had the real killer managed to get away without being seen. I frowned and tried to focus my attention on the Basin, searching for possible hiding places, but my head hurt too much and I gave up the effort. I had been careless, I chided myself. I had allowed myself to forget the dangerous game I was playing, and it had nearly cost me my life.

"What happened, Jenny?" Geoff spoke in that maddeningly cool tone.

I decided it was best to tell him nothing. "I was careless and slipped on the rocks and fell. Not too co-ordinated of me," I ventured. Then I asked a question of my own. "How did you happen to be up here?"

He looked at me for a long time before he said briefly, "Lynn asked me to come up and give you a ride down so you wouldn't be late for dinner. Do you think you can walk? We'd better get you to the Castle and have that cut looked after. It's rather a bad one."

I stood up slowly. The jeep was parked on the road a few hundred yards away. I was a little unsteady, but I gritted my teeth, determined not to show it. He stood beside me, waiting patiently. I took a step toward the jeep and almost collapsed. In falling I had managed to twist my ankle. Sharp needles of pain shot through my foot as I tried to put my weight on it. I winced and valiantly took another step.

Instantly, Geoff's arm was around my waist. "Jenny?" This time he managed to sound a little concerned.

"I think I sprained my ankle."

Without saying anything, he picked me up and carried me to the jeep. When he had deposited me on the seat, he reached into the glove compartment and brought out a flask. "Here," he said, "you look like you need some."

I took the flask and unscrewed the top. Experimentally, I took a sip thinking of all the grade-B movies I had seen where people are poisoned. I recognized the taste of Chivas Regal immediately. Another two sips and I put the cap on and handed it back to him. "Thanks," I told him wanly. "You seem to think of everything."

"Except getting puppies for little boys," he remarked quietly.

My head wasn't clear enough to even begin to decipher that.

———◆———

I lost consciousness somewhere on the road down the escarpment. When I came to again I was in my room at the Castle. Lynn was standing beside the bed, her face showing mixed concern and annoyance. "Well," she announced, "you're going to live it seems."

"So it seems," I agreed.

"Did you find what you were looking for?" she asked bitingly.

"No," I answered her with as much aplomb as I could manage. "Unfortunately, I didn't."

"You're going too far, Jenny. Let it alone. This time I mean it." Her eyes were cold, almost hostile.

I felt a wave of sadness that Lynn and I had come to this impasse. "Sorry." I tried to match her impersonal gaze but fell short.

"You were lucky this time. Next time you may not be so fortunate."

I took a deep breath. "Are you warning me or threatening me, Lynn?"

"Take it whatever way you want." She looked down at me, her lips in a tight line, her eyes hooded like Geoffrey's. I wondered suddenly why she had sent him after me.

The muffled roar of thunder came through the open window. An early evening storm was coming up, suddenly as they always do in the Colorado Rockies. Several gusts of wind caught the heavy velvet curtains and blew them back into the room, flaring them out so that they looked like huge green sails. Lynn crossed the room and quickly shut the windows. She looked out for a moment and then retraced her steps until she stood at the foot of the bed.

"What did you say to Paul this morning?" she demanded abruptly.

"Paul?" I echoed blankly.

"You must have told him something that made him change his mind."

I stared at her. My head was aching unmercifully. I didn't have the strength for this encounter Lynn seemed determined to force.

"I'm not blind and I'm not stupid, Jenifer. I know Paul far too well. Unfortunately, I know you far too little anymore. Now what did you tell him?" she demanded, her voice cutting like a whip.

"We discussed my father's affairs," I said wearily.

"You're lying, Jenny," Lynn countered evenly. "Just like you lied to Geoff about what happened to you. Paul is no more capable of deciding to come back to me with no questions asked than Geoff was of thinking of getting Christopher a dog. You've a fine hand, I'll say that for you, but you're a fool."

My last reserves of energy went. I had no strength, nor wit, left to fence with Lynn. All I wanted was to be left alone. To sleep. I closed my eyes.

"You're tired," Lynn said, her voice remaining matter-of-fact. "It can all wait for a few hours, I suppose. You'd better rest. I'll see that you're not disturbed."

She turned and with that graceful, lithe Cabot suppleness crossed to the door. She stood there a moment longer, the heavy brass knob in her hand, looking back at me. Then without speaking, she slipped through the door and was gone. Was it my imagination or did I hear a key turn in the lock? I was too exhausted to care. All I wanted was to be swept into some kind of oblivion where the pain would go away and I would be taken care of. I had narrowly escaped death, I told myself. The mere thought of it was chilling. It was one thing to have close calls that were the result of the accidental capriciousness of the universe. It was quite another to realize that someone—another human being—had coolly, maliciously tried to kill me. The knowledge was overwhelming.

Troubled, fretful, uneasy, I finally drifted to sleep.

———◆———

I spent the next day in bed. I wanted to get up but neither Lynn nor Elizabeth would hear of it. Lynn, quiet and somber, never saying much, stopped in every few hours, almost as if she were checking to make sure I was still alive. Elizabeth came more often, fussing over me, making sure I was comfortable, bringing me tall glasses of ice tea and plates of sandwiches and fresh-baked cookies. Even Kingston came by to inquire how I was feeling, to chide me a little for being so careless. Christopher and Strider came up and spent the afternoon with me. Christopher was open and friendly, acting more like a normal nine-year-old boy than I had ever seen him. I tried to ignore the nagging thought that I was beginning to care far too much for this boy who could never be mine. Leaving him, I feared, was going to be even harder than I had anticipated.

Bruce came just before dinner. He was gay and carefree, charming—all the things I had remembered him being.

"I know you're not feeling so great," he said finally, "so we won't talk about getting married until later. I've pacified Carole for a while, and Elizabeth will fix things up with her when we're ready."

I sighed inwardly. The subject I had wanted to avoid was in front of me. In my absorption with the deadly puzzles that surrounded Castle Cabot I hadn't thought much about Bruce in the past three days. I had been relieved that he'd left me alone. Not exactly the sort of behavior I should be exhibiting if I were really in love with him, I realized. I thought again of him pleading with me to marry him. Quite inexplicably Geoff's solemn, melancholy face flashed through my memory. I looked at Bruce. He was smiling at me; his blond hair was falling into his eyes. Carole had trapped him, I saw. He was a philanderer unable to flirt; a charming, whimsical playboy. His easy, smooth assurance seemed empty, a facade with nothing behind it. Other men— Paul, Geoff—they were different. I realized that I had wasted years of my life running away from something that no longer mattered.

"Bruce, listen to me." I looked at him steadily. "I'm different now. I want different things than I did ten years ago. I'm not in love with you. I'm not going to marry you. I'd like us to be friends. You're easy and charming when you're not pressing and you can be good company, but that's all I want from you. I'm sorry." I was firm but gentle. I felt sad.

"Come on, Jenny," he laughed. "You can't mean that. You still respond to me. You can't deny that."

"I'd never been foolish enough to deny that you're a very attractive man, Bruce, but that's not enough."

The laugh faded and his face took on a stricken look. "You can't do this to me, Jenny. I'm counting on you."

I shook my head. "Be honest, Bruce. For once, be honest. You don't care about me except as a way of getting something you want. Don't argue with me," I said a bit sharply when I could see him starting to speak. "It won't do any good."

His mouth tightened in a hurt, almost pouting line. He stared at me for several minutes and then without a word turned and left the room.

I sank back into the pillows. It was over, I thought with relief. I was free of Bruce Cabot at last. Then my relief faded as the throbbing in my head reminded me that I was still deeply entangled in the lives of the rest of the Cabots.

Someone had tried to kill me. I wanted somehow to reassure myself that the masked figure hadn't been Geoff. I reasoned that since I hadn't heard my assailant, it couldn't have been Geoff for surely I would have heard the jeep. The killer had to be someone else. Still, I was faced with the knowledge that only Geoff and Lynn had known where I was going and only Lynn knew why. Geoff had found me—Lynn had sent him. That left me with two possible conclusions. Either Lynn and Geoff were in collusion, or else neither of them was responsible—and one of the other Cabots was watching me. Only how had the killer gotten away? Geoff would have seen another jeep or a horse. That left the Mithral Stair. I heard again Angus telling me about the rotten timbers and blasted tunnels. He'd been so positive that no one had been on it since Philip Cabot's death. I'd accepted that at the time and seeing the rock-choked tunnel adits in the Basin had reinforced my acceptance. Now, I wasn't quite so sure. Perhaps most of the Stair was closed off, but I was willing to wager that a few of the tunnels were still safe. It explained a lot of things. How Christopher's saddle with its cut cinch could have disappeared; where the killer had gone. I decided to try to find the one open tunnel adit that would lead to the Stair. If I could find the saddle or the black garb the killer wore, I would be able to confront the Cabots with some evidence.

I slept restlessly again that night. Geoffrey Cabot's cold, stony face and ice-blue eyes ran through my dreams. I would awake periodically, with a start, my head throbbing, bathed in sweat.

CHAPTER 8

The next day, although my ankle was still sore, my headache was better and I decided to put my plan into action by riding up to Rob Roy Basin to look again for the entrance to the Mithral Stair. This time, however, I wouldn't advertise what I was doing. Letting Elizabeth think I was going up to my room to rest, I slipped out of the house and limped down to the stables. I saddled the chestnut mare I had ridden before and rode up the overgrown steep path I had climbed that first day I had met Christopher.

Once I'd reached the top of the Falls I turned away from the jeep road and began to reinspect the tunnel adits, thinking that perhaps it would be possible to get past the obstructing piles of rock. With each one I decided that my idea was not a good one. I rode as far as the ruins of the Rob Roy and then turned back to look down the Basin. Nothing. The tunnels from this point in the Basin were no longer blocked by rock slides. Instead, sagging timbers outlined a few feet of hewn rock and then there was simply blackness. I shuddered a little. I had never liked being underground. On the few occasions in childhood when I had been taken into the mines I had fought to control my fear of the narrow, damp-smelling lanes that ran into the roots of the mountains. I wasn't normally claustrophobic. Crowded elevators didn't bother me, nor did subways, but mine tunnels were something else again. I couldn't explain it, but I dreaded them.

All the remaining tunnels along the north wall of the Basin had been abandoned. The wooden ties from the rail tracks lay one after another, leading from the dumps back into the tunnels, mute but eloquent testimony of the activity that had once taken place here. None of them looked as though they could lead to the Mithral Stair. Disappointed and frustrated by the seeming impossibility of coming to grips with any of the puzzles that confronted me, I nudged the mare and began to pick my way across to the road. The ruins of the Rob Roy Mine were behind me, a mass of grayish tumbled rocks glistening in the sun. Rob Roy Creek tumbled through the center of the ruins. Except for the occasional sound of a rock falling as the fat, brown woodchucks scurried to and fro, and the hushed murmur of the stream, it was a wild deserted place.

I stayed on the road now, letting the mare plod steadily toward a narrow break in the sheer, impenetrable line of the peaks that bordered the south side of the Basin. There was an alpine lake there, I remembered, and I decided to ride to it. I leaned forward on the saddlehorn and let my mind ponder the multiple series of mysteries I had stumbled across when I had come to Castle Cabot. I was certain the Mithral Stair was still in use. But where was it? I was overlooking something in my search for it.

The lake was farther than I'd remembered. When at last I came to it, the road forked, a branch going to either side. I chose the right fork which hugged the base of the mountains. I rode to the end of the lake and then dismounted, tied the mare to a tree and limped down to the edge of the water. I stayed there a long time, watching the fish jump after flies, letting my thoughts wander.

The sun disappeared, but I paid no attention until I heard the distant roll of thunder. Startled, I looked up to discover that the sky had darkened. Masses of jet black clouds swarmed over the mountains. The thunder sounded frequently, getting louder each time. I looked anxiously for lightning but could see none. One thing I didn't want to do was get caught far up in the San Juans during a lightning storm.

I limped as fast as I could back to the mare. Before I had ridden around the lake, the storm broke. The clouds hung at the tops of the mountains cutting off almost all the natural light.

Grayish-white mist swirled down the sides of the peaks. The hail fell forcefully, in visible sheets. Soon, I could no longer see the other side of the lake. The meadows were quickly coated with white, the green blades of grass sticking up between the small particles of hail.

I shivered with the cold. Foolishly, I had taken no jacket with me and the thin sleeves of my shirt were no protection against the chill. The hail bounced as it hit me, stinging and making me even colder. I hunched over the mare and hoped that she wouldn't slip on the wet ground.

The thunder pealed constantly now, reverberating and echoing between the walls of the Basin. In the background, I could hear an occasional sound of rocks falling as parts of the overhanging rock ledges were loosened by the exploding sounds. I had just reached the fork in the road when the center of the storm moved over me. A huge crack of thunder tore across the sky directly overhead.

The next thing I knew I was on the wet, soggy ground—the mare, frightened by the thunder, was galloping madly toward Rob Roy Basin. Shaken, I stood up cursing myself. Lynn had been right. I was both foolish and careless. If before my situation had been unpleasant, it was now grim indeed. With my sprained ankle I was in no condition to walk the distance to the Castle—certainly not over the treacherously wet terrain. But walk I would have to. There was no other way of getting back. Gingerly, I began to pick my way along the road, trying to avoid the rivelets of water streaming down the ruts. With each step sharp needles of pain shot through my ankle.

The hail showed no signs of letting up and I was beginning to feel slightly numb. I looked around for sheltered places but could find none. After thirty minutes I had managed to walk about half a mile. I was cold. My fingers had very little feeling left in them and it was only with intense effort that I could bend them. My clothes were wet, and my hair was plastered to my head. I tried concentrating on the road, making sure I didn't slip, but I kept hearing King's voice telling me, "These mountains are treacherous, my dear. We did everything we could."

Was this how my father had died? Injured, alone, in one of the many wild basins that dotted the San Juans. I wondered if I had been on the wrong track all along. Perhaps my father had nothing to do with whatever was wrong at Castle Cabot.

The thunder still roared overhead. It wasn't as loud as the sky-splitting clap that had left me stranded, but it rumbled and echoed as frequently as before. Suddenly, I thought I heard a voice calling my name. Overactive imagination I told myself. A few steps later I heard it again and then was nearly knocked over by the horseman who appeared unexpectedly, seeming to materialize out of the swirling mist and driving hail.

It was Geoff.

He was riding my mare. As soon as he saw me, he pulled the mare to a halt and jumped off, keeping one of the reins tight in his hand. His eyes swept over me, registering every detail of my bedraggled appearance.

"So," he said rather ominously, "I've found you at last."

A shiver ran through me. He didn't wait for me to say anything but motioned toward the horse with the reins. "Get on."

Cold, stiff and more than a little numb, I somehow managed to haul myself into the saddle. Geoff handed me one of the reins, gruffly ordering me to hold onto it. Then he slipped my foot from the stirrup, inserted his own and swung up behind me. The mare flinched at the extra weight, her ears back indicating her displeasure. Geoff took the reins in his right hand, his left arm encircling my waist, holding me back against him.

Carefully, he urged the reluctant mare down the road. The hail was falling steadily although it had lost some of its ferocity. After riding perhaps ten minutes, he turned the horse onto a path than ran off to the right of the main road. Another ten minutes brought us to a small notch in the basin wall. Through the mist I could see a cabin, almost obscured by a stand of fir trees. Geoff dismounted and quickly tied the mare to one of the rails of a corral which stood beside the cabin. Stiffly, I got off, stumbling as I did so, falling against him. He steadied me for a second and then led the way to the cabin.

The door opened creakingly, groaning on its hinges. I expected to see a rundown shack, but surprisingly this cabin had been kept up. It was clean. A stack of wood lay beside a pot-bellied stove. Two rude wooden bunk beds were in one corner and in another was a pile of straw. The light was dim, filtering in through two small, almost opaque windows. A rickety looking wooden table was underneath the windows and on it was a kerosene lamp.

Efficiently and without speaking, Geoff built a fire in the stove. I stood, my back against the door, watching him, admiring his quick, sure movements, yet at the same time a bit fearful of his brooding silence. Finally, I decided to break the uneasy tension I could feel building up between us. "I didn't notice this cabin when I was riding up," I commented, thinking that I sounded a bit inane trying to make small talk to Geoffrey Cabot in such a situation. Still, I continued. "What's it for?"

"Forest Service cabin," he replied briefly without looking at me.

"Will we stay here long?"

"Until the storm stops. The mare should only ride one, so I'll have to walk down. I don't relish doing that in this hail." He had said nothing to reproach me, but I was stung by the cold, almost bitter tone of his voice. The fire was beginning to crackle in the stove, the metal popping as it heated up. "You'd better come over here and dry out," he ordered tersely.

Grateful for the suggestion I obeyed him. "I can't tell you how glad I was to see you. The mare was startled by a burst of thunder and threw me. I wasn't looking forward to walking back."

He said nothing but walked over, opened the door and peered out. Then he disappeared outside for a moment and returned carrying the saddle and saddle blanket. He dropped them on the floor and closed the door, kicking at the bottom of it.

It suddenly occurred to me to wonder how he had found me. No one had known where I was going. I had made sure that no one had seen me leave the Castle and had used the old trail to avoid being seen on the jeep road. "How did you know where I was?" I asked trying to keep the suspicion out of my voice.

He looked at me disgustedly, but again said nothing. Irritated,

I lashed out at him. "Dammit, Geoff! Can't you say anything? You have to be the most . . ." I sputtered to a stop, unable to think of an adjective to describe his chilly inaccessibility.

He turned toward me then, that sardonic look on his face. "What would you have me say, Jenny? That you do the stupidest things. Anyone would think you'd never lived around here. First, you stand too close to the edge of a waterfall and slip on the rocks, damn near killing yourself. Then with a sprained ankle you take off riding back into the mountains without telling anyone where you're going." He was ice cold, his blue eyes boring into me. I wished that he would be angry. Anything but this glacial contempt. "You don't take the proper clothes and let your horse get away from you in the middle of a hail storm. If I hadn't seen the mare coming down out of Rob Roy and followed the tracks back up here you could have died of exposure."

"I'll be eternally grateful," I told him sarcastically, stung by his criticism. Somehow we always seemed to be at each other's throats. I felt the need to hurt him and, before I could stop myself, I heard my own voice challenging him. "Still, it's strange isn't it, how you always manage to turn up. It's almost as though you're following me."

He laughed harshly. "Don't be ridiculous. Why would I waste my time?"

That angered me even more. "I'm sure you're aware that I didn't slip the other day. Someone tried to push me over the Falls. You and Lynn were the only ones who knew where I'd gone." I tried to match his cold, deadly tone.

He came closer to me, and as I moved away from the stove he backed me against the wall of the cabin. He loomed in front of me, his hands pressed against the wall, effectively caging me to the spot. "Are you suggesting that I'm trying to kill you?"

That strange tension ran between us once again. I looked at him, trying hard to remain calm, to still the riot of emotions I felt. My heart was beating rapidly and I could feel the blood pulsing in my wrists. "It's a possibility, isn't it," I told him frostily, wondering why I could always rouse him with this insinuation.

"So you've managed to suggest on several occasions, while on others you've indicated that you trust me. Which is it, Jenny?" He was grim.

I didn't know how to answer him. I realized that I was both afraid of him and attracted to him. I had no simple response when it came to Geoff. I skirted his question. "If you recall, you've never bothered to deny it. In fact, you've rather encouraged me to believe it."

I could see a muscle in his jaw twitching spasmodically. "Do I really frighten you that much?"

Something strange in his voice made me temporize my answer. "Sometimes. You shut yourself off from everyone, Geoff. No one knows how you feel or what you're thinking. What's unknown is frightening."

He was quiet for a moment and I thought perhaps he was going to soften, but instead a cruel smile flitted across his lips and there was a light in his eyes that I hadn't seen before. He drummed his forefinger against the wall and bent a little closer toward me.

"So you want to know me better, Jenny. Well perhaps that can be arranged."

Once again I was frightened of him. Determined not to let it show, I kept my voice steady. "I'm not sure I understand what you mean."

He held the cruel, mocking glance for a moment longer and then it faded abruptly, leaving only the closed, brooding face I had come to know all too well. "Forget it," he said dropping his hands and moving away from me.

Something compelled me not to let the matter drop. I followed him across the room. "Geoff," I began, not entirely sure of what I was going to say.

He turned suddenly and the next thing I knew I was in his arms. His lips were on mine, hard and insistent. He wasn't cruel the way he had been in the library, just unyielding, demanding. The force of his kisses left me unable to catch my breath. I knew that this was where we had been heading from the moment he had stood in the door of my hotel room and I wondered at myself for not realizing it sooner. It was what we both needed to burn away all the bleak years behind us. And, I admitted, it was what I wanted. I responded to Geoff, returning each embrace with a demanding urgency that matched his own.

Then, as suddenly as he had begun the embrace, he broke it, pushing me away from him. He walked several paces toward the stove. He pulled a cigarette out of his pocket and lit it. I stayed where I was, watching him as he smoked, saying nothing. His dark hair fell onto his forehead and he reached up, brushing it away. I could see the muscles in his face and throat move as he inhaled.

"You behave very strangely for someone who thinks I'm trying to murder her," he said finally. There was bitterness in his voice.

I didn't answer him right away. My basic dilemma hadn't changed. I walked over to him, reached up and ran my hand along the side of his face and let sentiment speak for me. "It doesn't matter."

"Doesn't it?"

"No. Not really."

He stared at me with an odd expression on his face—one I couldn't read. He dropped his cigarette on the floor and carefully ground it out with his toe. Then he closed his eyes for a moment as though he were in pain. Opening them, he slowly leaned down, his lips brushing softly over mine. I held my breath, wondering what he would do next. This was the last sort of behavior I would have expected from him. Which one was the real Geoffrey, I wondered, the grim, brooding man who had found me in the storm, the cruel almost evil man who had tried to frighten me, the hard, unyielding lover, or this one?

He gathered me into his arms and held me close. His hands moved across my back in firm stroking motions, almost like someone stroking a cat. His lips moved against my hair. I leaned against him, drawing warmth from his body, waiting placidly. At last I heard him groan. "Damn you, Jenny."

He held me away from him and once again his mouth found mine.

CHAPTER 9

I was drifting in a sort of euphoric limbo. I didn't care about any of the mysteries any longer. All that seemed to matter was the small, circumscribed world that surrounded the two of us. I wondered when I had fallen in love with Geoff. My infatuation with Bruce had been nothing compared to the depth of emotion I felt now. I smiled and snuggled my head deeper into the hollow of Geoff's shoulder. His chin rested against my hair so I couldn't see his face, but I could feel his arm draped loosely around me and I could hear the measured thud of his heart beneath my ear.

The room was a little lighter now, and though I strained to listen, I couldn't hear the hail falling on the roof. Everything was silent except for an occasional pop from the dying embers in the stove. The storm must have passed over. The hushed atmosphere fit my mood. I was relaxed and at peace for the first time I could remember.

It didn't last long. Soon, all too soon, I heard Geoff's voice coming from above my head. "The storm's over. We'd better go down before it gets too dark." I could tell nothing from his tone about how he felt. Nor, a moment later, when I saw his face did it reveal anything.

Finally, I said softly, "You didn't intend to do that, did you?"

He was scattering the coals in the stove, his back to me. "No," he said without turning. Then in a moment. "But don't expect me to apologize."

"I didn't ask you to," I told him evenly.

That made him look at me for a moment. "Take that bucket,"

he said, nodding at a pail sitting near the door, "and get some water from the spring."

I swallowed my hurt and disappointment and obeyed his directions without question. So that's how it's going to be, I thought woodenly. He doesn't care at all. It was a momentary lapse; something that shouldn't have happened. I meant nothing to him. I was a nuisance, an annoyance who would soon be gone and forgotten. Still, a small voice that I couldn't control whispered that I had made a crack in his granite surface.

I tried to ignore that insidious, wild hope. One couldn't live on hopes and dreams. Surely I had learned that painful lesson. But it took root and it would flourish. I knew myself well enough for that. And once again I would be hurt, and it would be no one's fault but my own.

Geoff was businesslike, dousing the fire with the bucket of water, making sure the door was closed tightly, checking the mare to see how she had fared during the storm, resaddling her. When he spoke, his voice was expressionless, his poker-faced mask firmly in place.

I rode the mare while Geoff took the reins and walked in front, leading her down the road. He walked briskly, as though he couldn't wait to get back. Trying to keep my mind off him, I began searching the side of Rob Roy Basin once again, looking for tunnel adits I might have missed. It wasn't until we reached the series of switchbacks that snaked down the escarpment to the Castle that I saw it. Half hidden behind a knobby protuberance on the south flank of Mithral Mountain was a tunnel entrance. It lay several hundred feet above the level of the tunnels I had been inspecting, so that I couldn't see it clearly, but now, from my vantage point, it seemed to be clear of debris. Suddenly, in spite of myself, I was excited. That's it, I thought confidently. That's the entrance to the Mithral Stair.

Nothing was said by the Cabots when Geoff and I arrived at the Castle. However, I noticed that Elizabeth gave us a long, speculative look, and Lynn let a worried frown cross her face before she caught herself. I expected her to find an opportunity to give me another warning, but she remained silent. Geoff disappeared with Kingston and I didn't see him again. I spent the evening upstairs with Christopher. The only interruption was a call from Paul asking me to come down in the morning.

I arrived at his office about nine o'clock. He was looking much better than the last time I had seen him. "I've got some of the information you wanted," he told me as I walked in.

"Great," I said, settling myself in the now familiar armchair. "Let's hear it."

"I still have a hard time believing all this, you know."

"Yes," I agreed. "I had trouble believing it too until someone tried to push me over the Falls the other day."

"What!" Paul's voice cracked across the room. "Lynn said it was an accident."

"It was supposed to look like one, but I didn't slip. Someone dressed in black, wearing one of those nylon face masks and gloves, tried to push me over."

"That's incredible! But why? With Christopher there's at least a reason—the will change. Why you?"

I decided it was time to tell Paul a little more. Just in case my luck turned, someone else should know the story. "I'm getting too close to the truth. It's more than just Christopher. As I mentioned the other day, I don't think my father got lost in the mountains. I think he was murdered because someone found out he had rigged Philip Cabot's fatal accident. I'm not totally sure why he wanted to kill Philip. It could have to do with my mother, and then again it could have to do with the Cottonwood land. According to Angus, Philip and my father were trying to find a strike up there. What did you find out?"

Paul didn't reply. Instead he sat, staring open-mouthed at me. I didn't blame him. The things I was talking about didn't happen in real life. But then things at Castle Cabot seemed very far from "real life."

"Paul," I prodded him.

"Sorry, Jenny. It's just—so unbelievable." He shook his head, his tousled hair falling in his eyes. "Well," he began, "about the land. As you know, it's not necessary to own the surface land in order to stake claims on the minerals. At one time the land apparently did belong to Philip Cabot, although he never filed the deed so there's no legal record that he owned it. He staked a couple of unpatented claims and worked them. I found the assessment papers. Then, after a few years, he let them go. Your father picked them up in 1950 and kept them until he died. Now they're up for grabs again. How he got the land itself I don't know. The deed is first recorded in his name in 1949.

Something was registering in the back of my mind. "You're sure that it was 1949?" I interrupted him.

"Yes."

The year before my mother died, I thought. Curious. Clearly he hadn't killed Philip Cabot for the land. It had been my mother after all. No wonder he hadn't wanted anything to do with me. "What about the stock?"

"King incorporated the Cabot holdings four years ago. That's a year before your father disappeared. Your father is the only non-Cabot to hold stock in the corporation. King gave it to him in appreciation for past services. He had five per cent of the stock. King holds fifty per cent, Elizabeth fifteen per cent, Bruce, Lynn and Geoff ten per cent each. "Now," Paul continued, picking up a piece of paper from his desk, "I did manage to find this in some old papers in the Colvada Mill."

He handed me an old, much folded piece of paper. It was a map of the Mithral Stair. It had been hand drawn I saw, each tunnel labeled in neat block letters. From my trips to Rob Roy Basin I could place some of the outlets to the Stair. The one I had seen yesterday, which had looked as though it might still be in use, was the Jackpot and it was on the fifth level. One more part of my father's note explained. I looked for the Grubstake tunnel and found it on the third level of the Stair. If Angus' description of the cave-in were accurate, the tunnel would be impassable. That left only the Flying Dutchman.

I bent over the map examining it closely. There was one tunnel that puzzled me. It looked as though it entered directly from the face of the escarpment. It was labeled "level one" and denoted as the Mithral Mine. That had been the original Cabot strike made a hundred years ago by the first Kingston Cabot. I had heard about the mine. It was a kind of local myth, but I never remembered knowing where the tunnel was. Then, quite suddenly, I had it.

"Of course," I breathed, "the Castle." I remembered Angus telling me that the second Kingston Cabot had built the Stair so he could go through the mountain. There had to be an entrance to the Stair in the library. It was the only room that ran along the back side of the Castle, abutting onto the rock of the escarpment.

Pieces began to fall into place. I had assumed that there would have to be at least two entrances to the Stair that were still in use, but it had never occurred to me that one of them would be in the Castle itself. Whoever was responsible for the attacks on Christopher and myself could slip onto the Stair without being seen or missed by the rest of the family. All I had to do was find the entrance.

———◆———

It was the next morning before I had a chance to examine the library. Finally, Carole and Bruce left to go riding and I was alone in the Castle. I seized the opportunity to search for the opening to the Stair. I confined my investigations to the back wall of the room. I went over it inch by inch, pressing, tapping, poking. None of them worked. Three more times I went over the same ground and each time with the same negative results. I was hampered by the fact that much of the wall was covered, floor to ceiling with built-in bookcases. It would be a monumental task to remove every volume. I tired to logically deduce where the second King Cabot would have put the door.

The operating mechanism probably wouldn't be higher than a man could reach. It would seem ridiculous to place it at the top of the bookcases. But it was possible that the opening device could have been built into the floor. With that idea in mind, I turned my attention to the wood paneling at the base of the wall, but again my search was fruitless. There was nothing to it, but to tackle the books. Several hours later, much begrimed and more than a little anxious lest one of the Cabots return, I had covered half of the bookcase.

I stood back, wiping my hand across my forehead, and stared at the remaining rows of books. Maybe I was wrong. It was outlandish to think that there would be a secret entrance to the Mithral Stair. No doubt there had been a tunnel that had been sealed when the house was built across it. The map may have simply been indicating its existence, not its usefulness. My eyes ranged over the titles and stopped on a volume which had the words *Flying Dutchman* etched on its spine. I stared at it. That's it, I thought. The last word in my father's message decoded. Pulling it out, I saw that it was a German libretto for the Wagner opera. Peering at the paneling behind the book I noticed a seam. Normally, the wooden panels ran without interruption from floor to ceiling, but this one was pieced. It was a tight fitting job, and if I hadn't happened to catch the right angle of light, I would have missed it. I removed two more books and reached in, holding my breath in anticipation of what I would find. Running my fingers along the seam where the two pieces of wood joined, I poked and pushed but this time with results. A small square of the panel, perhaps six inches on a side, popped open revealing a small, inset chamber and two buttons.

I pressed the top button and immediately heard a soft, almost indistinct whirring sound. Noiselessly, a large section of the bookcase slid back turning sideways, as it did so. A cold blast of damp, earthy smelling air wafted up from the opening. I breathed it in. There was nothing quite as unmistakable as the smell of the underground. A short flight of stone steps led down to a tunnel and in the inadequate light from the library I could see a wooden door a few hundred feet from the foot of the stairs.

I've found it, I exulted. I've found the Mithral Stair.

It was my excitement that made me incautious. Forgetting all need for watchfulness, forgetting the danger I was in if someone should find me here—forgetting even my fear of tunnels—I carefully negotiated the narrow steps and began to inspect the entrance to the Stair. It was well kept up. The timbers were solid, there was no loose rock from cave-ins on the floor of the tunnel. The door, which I could see only dimly, appeared to be heavy. It was padlocked shut. The big black lock looked new and had recently been oiled. I had been right. The Mithral Stair was far from abandoned.

Now my problem was how to get past the padlocked door. I could, of course, take a crowbar and try to pry the lock loose, but I didn't want to be so crude and obvious. If only I had a key. I could make an impression of the lock and go to a locksmith, but that would take time. Then it occurred to me that among my various perplexing legacies from my father had been two keys, one of which still had no lock. Perhaps, just perhaps, I thought, it was the key to this door. I determined to come back as soon as I could with the proper equipment to explore the tunnels.

I turned to go back to the library, satisfied with my day's accomplishments. I was convinced that I would have the answer to my questions soon. It was then that I noticed the lessening of light in the tunnel and looked up to see the doorway to the library silently sliding shut.

"No!" I cried out frantically. "No. Wait!"

My only answer was a low, rumbling laughter. I ran toward the closing door as the last pencil-thin sliver of light dwindled into blackness. I stumbled against the bottom step, banging my bad ankle. I cursed aloud as I caught myself from falling face first onto the hard edges of stone. Carefully, I sat down and rubbed my shin, while I tried vainly to calm my pounding heart. The blood throbbed in my ears, almost deafening me. I was trapped. Shut in. Left to die on the Mithral Stair. My old fear of being underground swept over me, threatening to overwhelm me. Desperately, I forced myself to think about my predicament.

How stupid I had been! I had given the killer the perfect chance. But, I shook myself, it did no good to think of that now. My task was to figure out how to get out of the tunnel. I had no doubt that I was meant to stay here, shut up in the Stygian blackness until I died. I shuddered a little at the thought of such a gruesome death.

Remembering from somewhere that people lose their sense of balance in total darkness, I painstakingly crawled up the stairs on my hands and knees. When I reached the top step, I began to feel very carefully over the surface of the door. The wood was cool and smooth against my hands. There were no buttons, no indentations, no cracks in the solid wooden wall that lay between me and the interior of Castle Cabot.

Frantic, I carefully stood up, making sure that I continually leaned against the corner where the tunnel wall joined the opening into the library. The stone of the tunnel was ice cold and I found myself shivering. I covered the top half of the door as I had the bottom, but again could discover no way of opening the panel. There had to be a way to operate the door from this side, of that I was sure. But I was equally sure that without light, I would never find it. Slowly, I sank back down on the top step and crouched there, huddled against the cool wood. I thought about dying. The air seemed fresh enough. I wouldn't die of suffocation but rather of starvation. A long, slow, painful process. I wanted to scream, but I knew it wouldn't do any good. No one would hear me, not through the thickness that divided me from the Castle.

Sternly, I took hold of myself. This would never do. I had to calm down, otherwise I would imagine myself into hysteria before anyone had a chance to rescue me. Surely, Lynn would come forward when she realized I had disappeared. She knew I knew about the Stair. Paul knew I had the map. They would say something. It was simply a matter of waiting. Unless, I thought uneasily, Lynn had been the one who had closed the panel. I hadn't imagined that laugh. It belonged to someone in the Castle. The door had been motor operated so it couldn't close accidentally. Someone had pressed that other button and had stood there laughing as the door slid shut. The same person who very deliberately tried to kill me before; who had tried to kill Christopher. I could trust none of them, I warned myself, least of all the ones I wanted to trust. The Cabots stood together against outsiders, and I for all their friendliness was an outsider. Maybe they would let me die here.

I thought then of Geoff, of those hours in the cabin during the storm, of the might have beens that never were. I slumped against the wall. Closing my eyes I resigned myself to whatever would happen.

———◆———

The door opened slowly. I became aware of it only when I felt the edge of the top step cutting into my ribs. Uncertain for a moment of where I was, I looked up with disbelief at the widening crack of light. It was so bright that I was squinting, my eyes almost shut. I didn't recognize the figure that bent over me until I heard Geoff's voice.

"Jenny. Jenny, are you all right?"

I smiled. I had never been so grateful to hear that smooth, cool, even voice as I was now. He bent down, put his hands under my arms and quickly lifted me up into the library. I was still unable to make the adjustment from total darkness to so much light. The others in the room were hazy outlines, patches of color. They didn't matter anyhow. All that mattered was Geoff. His arms were around me and his hand was moving through my hair as he murmured my name. I clung to him. In all the murky, fearful phantasmagoria of the past hours, my love for Geoff was the one solid thing I could count on. He couldn't be the murderer. He couldn't possibly. I loved him far too much.

Finally, another voice penetrated my consciousness. "What happened, Jenny?"

Reluctantly, I pulled away from Geoff. He kept his arm around me, as though to steady me. I looked at the other people in the room. King and Lynn stood nearby, and it was Lynn who was waiting for my answer. I decided to be less than truthful.

"It was so stupid," I tried to laugh it off. Miraculously, my voice was calm. "I was looking for something to read and happened to notice the panel in the wall. I guess my curiosity got the best of me, and when the wall opened up, I went down to see what was there. The door swung shut before I could get back." I wondered how long it would take the Cabots to realize I was having too many accidents.

Lynn grimaced in disgust. "Honestly, Jenny. How can you continually be so careless?"

"Now, Lynn." This was Kingston, gently reprimanding his daughter. "I'm sure Jenny has thought of that already." He turned to me. "You're all right?"

"Yes. Now. How did you ever figure out where I was?"

They all looked at each other. Finally, King explained. "We were concerned when you didn't come down for dinner and your car was still here. Christopher said he'd seen you in the library early this afternoon and then Lynn noticed that the *Flying Dutchman* had been moved, so we decided you had stumbled onto the panel."

So Lynn did know about the panel and the Stair, I thought. I had been right about that at least. "What's it for anyway?" I said innocently.

Lynn looked simultaneously uncomfortable and annoyed. "It used to be an entrance to the tunnels that honeycomb the mountains. It hasn't been used in years." King passed it off nonchalantly.

I wondered if he was deliberately lying or if he didn't know. Just then Elizabeth rushed through the doorway followed by Bruce and Carole. She stopped when she saw me. "Jenny, thank God. We were frantic." Her voice trembled slightly with concern. "What happened?" When King finished telling her she turned to him. "I had no idea that door still worked. No one has used it since—" she broke off.

King nodded somberly. "Yes, I know. I'll have it dismantled before something like this happens again. Thank heaven Chris saw her."

Lynn had moved over to the bar and now thrust a brandy into my hand. "Here, drink this. It'll brace you up." Geoff still had his arm around me and showed no signs of removing it. I saw Elizabeth, her sharp eyes missing nothing, take note of her older son's solicitousness. I wondered what she thought about it.

I sipped at the brandy. It burst in my throat and then plunged warmly to my stomach. As always when I drank cordials, an involuntary shiver ran through me. Geoff noticed it and his arm tightened around me. I smiled up at him. "It's all right," I assured him. "It's just the brandy."

My smile faded when I saw his face. Whatever he meant by keeping his arm around me, his face still bore that cool, distant look. His blue eyes were watchful, and if they seemed to have lost some of their ice, I told myself sternly that it was probably just my imagination. I moved out of the circle of his arm, drained the last of the brandy and set the glass down on the desk. I could be cool as well. My chin set in a determined line. I wasn't going to throw myself at him, ruefully realizing that that was exactly what I had done.

Bruce had gone over to examine the panel which still stood open, revealing the entrance to the Mithral Stair. "I never knew this was here," he said. "Where does it go?"

"Back into the mountain," Elizabeth answered him briefly.

Bruce was intrigued. "This is great!" he exclaimed delightedly. "You mean it leads to all the tunnels in the mountain. Secret passageways and all that. Too bad we didn't know about this when we were kids. When you get ready to be adventurous again, Jenny, I'll help you explore it."

"No one is going to explore it!" Elizabeth's voice exploded into the silence. Seldom had I heard her be so adamant. "The Stair has been closed off for years, and it's going to stay that way. Besides, it's dangerous. Kingston you *will* take care of that door." It was a command.

King had crossed to push the button to activate the motor. The door was closing and all eyes were on it as he replied. "Of course, dear. First chance I get."

"But, Elizabeth," Bruce protested.

Lynn cut in, her low voice carrying a hidden sense of urgency. "Don't be such an ass, Bruce. Let it be."

He turned on her angrily. "Now see here, Lynn, I won't be spoken to like that. Not even from you."

"Children!" King's reprimand echoed in the room. "Have a little bit of respect for your mother."

Bruce, thwarted, spun around to face his father. "What's Elizabeth got to do with it?"

King's brow furrowed in annoyance. Lynn put a hand out as if to dissuade her brother from continuing, but he shook it off. I flicked a quick glance at Geoff. He, at least, seemed to grasp the significance of the tunnel. After all, it had been his father and he had been there. I wondered how much he remembered.

Elizabeth moved forward, breaking the moment of tension. "It's all right, Kingston. I suppose you've forgotten or maybe you never knew, Bruce. That passageway leads to the tunnel where Philip was killed. It's been shut up ever since." Elizabeth had herself in hand again after her momentary lapse. Obviously, she still felt very strongly about her first husband. Quite suddenly, I found myself speculating if all these years King had been playing encore to a dead man.

Inaudibly, Bruce apologized to her, while Lynn, more grim than usual, picked up the books and placed them back on the shelf, covering the control box. The wall stood as it had this morning before I'd discovered the Stair, but the knowledge of what lay behind the panel changed my entire way of looking at the room. I would have to get back in there before King dismantled the motor and jammed the door shut forever. I felt sure that somewhere on the Mithral Stair was the proof I needed to show that one of the Cabots was a murderer. But which one? I looked at each familiar face. Any of them could have done it, I realized, even Geoff.

CHAPTER 10

Elizabeth took me into the kitchen where she warmed up some roast beef and vegetables and quickly tore up lettuce for a salad. Watching her, I realized how hungry I was. She seemed extremely nervous but didn't say anything to me until I'd finished eating. Then she suggested that we go outside. She wanted to talk to me she said. Wondering what she had in mind, I followed her. She led the way to Mithral Falls. Once there I waited patiently as she paced back and forth. It was as though she were trying to nerve herself for what she was going to say. Finally, her back turned toward me, she straightened and began.

"Jenny, I'm going to be brutally frank with you. This is something I've never done before, not even with Kingston, but I hope to save you from making a terrible mistake." She turned to face me and smiled wearily.

"You're in love with Geoffrey," she plunged in. "I could see it in your face tonight in the library. I don't know why you are. God knows, Geoff never does anything to make any of us love him—" She broke off and continued in a different vein. "You've done wonders for Christopher, and Geoff seemed to be taking an interest in him. I almost allowed myself to think that it was all over, but," she shook her head vigorously, "it was too much to hope for. He'll never change." There was a flat note of hopelessness in her voice. I realized I was seeing a side of Elizabeth few people knew. Still, whatever she was hinting at, I was going to force her to come out in the open and say it.

"I'm afraid I don't quite understand, Elizabeth."

"I'm ashamed to say that Geoff is a cold, cruel, sometimes sadistic man. Part of it is my fault. I was young when I married Philip. Young and selfish. I was madly in love with him and I didn't want to share him with anyone—not even a son. When Geoff was born, Philip was delighted. He doted on him. I resented Geoff because he took Philip away from me. Then, after the accident I couldn't bear the sight of Geoff. You never knew Philip, but Geoff looks so like him. It was too painful. All these years I've ignored him. It wasn't until Nancy that I began to realize what I'd done.

"Nancy was a soft, sweet girl, very much in love with him. Very young and unprotected. I never knew why he married her. I don't think he ever cared about her. The way he treated her was unspeakable. He drove her away from him finally. Bruce and Carole weren't getting along, so Nancy turned to Bruce. It was—very messy, to say the least. Kingston and I convinced her that it was best to go away, but Geoff forced her to leave Christopher behind. And you've seen how he is with him." She reached out and grabbed my hands. I could feel the urgency straining behind her fingers.

"I know this must be difficult for you, Jenny, but you must leave here before you get any further involved. You'll only get hurt. Geoff is incapable of caring for anyone. The realization of how much I'm responsible for that has been my burden these past years." Her face was a shadowed mask of despair as she finished. For the first time, Elizabeth looked her age. Her shoulders were slumped forward; her large body seemed too big for her.

I was stunned. I had never heard Elizabeth be so candid about her children, and had never seen her like this. She was right of course. Geoff was a cold imperious bastard. I had said it all to myself many times, but I had chosen to ignore it, thinking that I could see signs of him softening.

"Don't try to fool yourself into thinking you can change him," Elizabeth warned wearily, reading my thoughts perfectly. "Nancy tried that."

When I didn't answer, she pressed again. "I'm afraid for you. I never know what Geoff will do. He's always known about the panel. I'm sure he shut you in there to frighten you. That door doesn't close by itself. It has to be motor-activated. Once, when Nancy was pregnant, he caught her with Bruce and tried to kill her. He's always thought Chris was Bruce's son. That's why he hates him so. He's dangerous, Jenny. You must leave at once."

I didn't know what to say. Elizabeth, having bared her anguish, was staring at me, tensely awaiting my answer. "I don't know," I said finally, withdrawing my hands from her. "I'll have to think about it."

She straightened and stepped back, her face slipping into its familiar graceful expression. She was the old Elizabeth again— the one I had always known. "Of course, dear. Just don't take too long."

Once in my room I went over everything Elizabeth had said, nodding assent at every turn. Yes. Yes. Geoff was like that. But he was also something else. I remembered the odd note in his voice when he had promised to get the dog for Christopher, the way he had restrained himself from striking me on the mountain and his gentleness when we had made love. Elizabeth was probably right. But she was wrong too. I cursed myself for not listening to reason. It was folly to think that I could do anything with Geoff, that I could give him something Nancy hadn't. I had been foolish enough over one of the Cabot men, and it was about time I started exhibiting some sense. Besides, Geoff could well be the one who had shut the panel. I had no reason to rule him out except for my strong feelings that he couldn't be the killer. He certainly had as many motives as any of the others. I sat on the bed and put my head in my hands. Give it up, Jenny, I thought. The tangled morass of life and death at Castle Cabot wasn't my problem. My life had grown away from Kingsville, from anything that might have happened to my father. It didn't matter any more. Elizabeth was right. I should leave. With sudden decision I pulled the suitcase out of the closet and flipped it open. I would pack and be gone tonight, before I could see anyone, before I could change my mind.

There was a knock at the door. Startled, I warily walked over and opened it quickly, not knowing who I would find. Christopher, looking very small and vulnerable in his blue-striped pajamas, stood there with Strider sitting patiently behind him.

"Chris. What on earth are you doing up at this hour? Is something wrong?"

"I thought you might want company, so Strider and I came to stay with you. Do you mind?" He sounded very adult and yet appealingly childish at the same time. He stood looking up at me, and I had to turn away to hide the sudden spurt of tears that threatened to overwhelm me.

He came into the room and closed the door, moving so that he stood in front of me. "It's all right, Jenny," he consoled, taking my hand. "Nothing can happen to you. Strider's a good watchdog." He made the assertion stoutly.

I swallowed with difficulty unable to speak.

Then he saw the suitcase. "You're going to go away," he cried. I could hear the fear and uncertainty in his voice, so different from the solemn, adult tone he'd had a moment before. One look at his face decided me. I swept the suitcase up and placed it carefully back in the closet. Despite what might happen to me, despite Geoff, I couldn't leave while there was a chance that by my presence I could safeguard Christopher.

I knelt and put my hands on his shoulders. "I was thinking about it," I told him frankly, "but that's all over now. I'm not going to leave you. I promise you." I didn't know how I was going to keep that rash pledge, but seeing the gladness flash across his face I knew that I would find a way somehow. Even if it meant taking him away with me.

◆

Elizabeth didn't seem surprised the next morning when I told her that I had decided to stay. I offered to move back to Angus' if it would be more comfortable for the Cabots. She turned me down, as I'd hoped she would, and with a discouraged shrug she told me, "It's your life, Jenny. I only hope for all our sakes you know what you're doing with it. I've tried to make you see reason."

"I know," I hastily assured her. "I'm prepared to take the consequences."

◆

I knew that Elizabeth would be at the Castle for most of the day and that I would have no chance of getting back to the Stair, so I sought Bruce out and told him I wanted to talk to him. I wanted to hear his version of what had happened with Nancy Cabot. I had no doubt that Elizabeth believed what she had told me, but I thought that perhaps she had been given a slanted version of events. I also wanted to know if Christopher was indeed Bruce's son. Perhaps Bruce could shed some light on the motivations of some of the Cabots. I suggested we go riding up Cottonwood. I wanted to make sure there was no possibility of being overheard. I also hoped that by turning my attention away from the Stair I could lull the killer into a false sense of security.

We rode companionably up the creek. Bruce was being good company today. He seemed to have taken my refusal well. I was surprised and pleased. He was gay and relaxed, clowning and showing off the way I remembered him. About halfway up the canyon we dismounted, tied the horses to a nearby tree and sat down on the soft alpine grass by the stream.

"Bruce," I began, "what happened between you and Geoff's wife?"

He threw his head back and laughed. "Digging up old skeletons, Jenny?"

"Just curious. It seems to be common gossip that the two of you had an affair. I just wanted to hear your side."

"Sure. I had a fling with Nancy. Carole and I were bored with each other and she had started making a play for Geoff. Nancy came to me to ask if I wouldn't do something about it. I was nice to her, and the rest was easy. She was an impressionable girl. Romantic type."

"Is Christopher your son, then?"

He looked at me, amused lights dancing in his eyes. "Of course not. All you have to do is look at him. Geoff seems to think so at times because Nancy kept trying to make him jealous, taunting him with the question of Chris' paternity, but he's Geoff's all right."

"Did she succeed? In making Geoff jealous, I mean."

"It's hard to tell. You know Geoff. Once she made him angry though. One of the few times I've ever seen Geoff lose his temper."

"Was that when he caught the two of you together?"

Again Bruce hooted with laughter. "You have been listening to stories." He sobered a little. "So you want to know all about it, Jenny. Okay. It was about four years after Geoff brought Nancy to Kingsville. Christopher was two or three I guess. Nancy and I had been having a fling off and on since right after Chris was born. Anyway, she was pregnant again and Geoff was sure this one was mine. As a matter of fact, it probably was. He found us together and he was furious. They argued and at some point he hit her. She stumbled backward and fell down the stairs. She had a miscarriage and almost died. That was when Elizabeth and King convinced her she should leave."

I went limp with relief. I had been listening to Bruce, my body tense, waiting to absorb the shock of having my doubts about Geoff confirmed. But it *had* been an accident. A real accident this time. He had been angry, wanted to hurt her no doubt, but he hadn't deliberately set out to kill her as Elizabeth had implied.

Bruce was lazily tossing small rocks into the stream. He threw one into the air and squinted into the sun following it. "So," he said almost offhandedly, "when are you and Geoff going to get married?"

I forced a smile. "You've a vivid imagination, Bruce."

"Not really. It seems pretty clear what's going on. I'm not sure I like being turned down for my half-brother." He said this almost petulantly.

"You should know Geoff well enough to realize that he's not interested in me or in any woman." My heart sank as I said it because I feared that it was the truth.

"That doesn't mean you're not interested in him. What is it? It shouldn't be the money. You'll have enough of your own after you sell this land."

"It bothers you, doesn't it, that King changed his will?" I countered.

"Of course it bothers me. The mines should come to me regardless. They've always gone to the eldest son. It doesn't matter that I've no heirs. My God," he protested, "I'm barely thirty." He had fallen back into that boasting, demanding, spoiled tone that I hated.

"Why don't you and Carole go ahead and have a child. King would probably change his will back again."

"It won't work," he declared flatly.

"Why not? Carole wants the money as much as you do. Certainly she'd be willing to have a baby to get it. The Cabots are rich enough to hire nurses. She wouldn't even have to take care of it."

He stood up, lifted a large rock in one hand and flung it into the creek. It cracked hollowly against the other boulders already in the stream bed. "She can't," he said finally in a somber tone.

I digested that. At last I understood the canker that had been driving at least some of the Cabots. Bruce and Carole had been driven apart by their own arrogant natures, developing their strange love-hate pattern. Bruce wanted an heir; Carole couldn't have one. His ardor for her would have cooled. Carole would never admit that she was unable to have children. Instead, she haughtily let it be known that she didn't want children and everyone had believed her. King, trying to force their hand, had changed his will, not knowing that it would do no good. Knowing that it didn't matter and that her advances would never lead anywhere, Carole had taunted Bruce by her flirtations with Geoff. Bruce, in turn, had countered with Nancy. It was a game of oneupsmanship.

Bruce's voice broke into the stream of my thoughts. "Carole and I could get along until King changed the will. We're a lot alike I guess. It probably wouldn't have worked out between you and me anyway, Jenny. I thought it would be fun to play around with you, and then when I found out about your land I thought that if I could get you to marry me I wouldn't have to worry about the Cabot money. But it's just as well you said no, although I admit it was a blow to my ego. Carole's the only one I've ever really wanted. But now King's made it impossible. Carole and I can't live without money. I've got to be the heir, Jenny. Surely you see that. It's my whole life."

He was looking at me with a solemn, serious expression. I found that I was touched. I hadn't suspected that Bruce could be so candid and honest about himself. I wanted to help him.

"You might," I suggested practically, "tell King why you haven't had any children. Once he knows I'm sure he'd leave you the mines on the condition that at your death it all passes to Christopher."

Bruce thought about this for a moment and then his face broke into a broad smile. "Jenny!" he exclaimed delightedly. "You've got it. You're terrific!"

He moved suddenly—as though to give me a kiss—so that he was directly in front of me. Everything happened so quickly then. I saw a strange look come over his face. He stumbled and then I heard the cracking echo of the rifle. Instinctively, I threw myself to the ground, rolling over so that I was partially concealed by a large boulder that stood beside the creek. I looked up at Bruce. It was then that I knew the depth of horror that had awaited me at Castle Cabot.

It was like a slow-motion picture. Bruce was trying to stand, but his knees kept buckling underneath him. His blue polo shirt was rapidly turning red. His mouth was slightly open, a red trickle of blood ran slowly out of the corner and down his chin. His eyes were wide and glassy with disbelief. I bit my lip. There was nothing I could do but watch him as he fell, softly and somehow oddly graceful.

I waited a few long, agonizing moments, expecting to hear the spang of the rifle again, but it was quiet. Bruce's breathing was shallow. I could barely see his chest move. I knew I had to get help.

I had no idea if the killer was sitting somewhere waiting for me to move so that he would have a shot, or if, having missed me and hit Bruce instead, he had escaped. I decided to take no chances. Gradually, inch by inch, I crawled Indian fashion toward the road and the horses, being careful to keep shielded behind rocks, bushes, any sort of cover I could find. Once I reached the trees, I stood up and dashed for the horses, my back stiffened, waiting for the shock of the bullet. None came. Quickly, I untied Bruce's bay gelding and mounted. The big horse would be faster than my mare, although I sensed that speed was futile. Bruce would be dead by the time I reached anyone. Still, I kicked the gelding into a gallop and we rushed headlong down the creek.

It probably took about twenty minutes to cover the distance to the Colvada mill, but to me it seemed forever. All I could see was the stunned look on Bruce's face. I prayed that someone would be at the mill. King or Geoff. It didn't matter. Just someone with whom I could share this intolerable burden.

I raced into the mill yard, pulled the bay up short and leapt off. As luck would have it, Geoff was standing on the steps leading up to the office. "Quick!" I gasped before he could say anything. "Up Cottonwood. Bruce. He's been shot." My voice broke, but with an effort I held myself together.

There was a stunned moment of silence. Then Geoff ran into the office and reappeared a moment later with a first-aid kit and some blankets. He took my hand and pulled me toward the jeep. Shouting at one of the men to take care of the horse, Geoff slammed the jeep into gear and it jumped forward, spewing gravel out behind. "I called Don Mason," Geoff told me. "He'll follow us up."

I nodded mutely. Neither of us spoke during the interminable drive back up the creek. Geoff drove expertly, clenching the steering wheel so tightly that his knuckles were white as he piloted the jeep up the narrow, winding dirt road. Once he reached out and grasped my hand for a moment, reassuringly.

I looked at him and tried to smile. It was a weak effort. I was grateful for his instinctive understanding that I needed a while to compose myself before I could explain what had happened.

My mare was still tied to the tree. Hurriedly, I led Geoff down to the small clearing by the creek. Bruce lay as I had left him, his body slightly twisted, his brown eyes wide in disbelief. A soft breeze caught at loose strands of his blond hair and brushed them down over his forehead. He had fallen beside one of the numerous small pools of rain water that become trapped in hollows in the rock. His blood had seeped into the pool, turning it carmine. Already a few big Colorado horseflies were beginning to hover over sticky moist places in the soil.

Geoff looked at him wordlessly, then he stooped down and closed the staring eyes. "Jenny." Geoff came over to stand in front of me. "Can you tell me what happened?"

All I could think of was that it shouldn't be Bruce who lay there. I knew that the shot had been intended for me, and that by a fantastic quirk of fate, Bruce had moved unexpectedly into the path of the bullet. It was a sobering thought. So close. I looked up at Geoff and his eyes steadied me.

"We had ridden up the canyon and had stopped here to talk. Bruce was standing throwing rocks in the stream. I heard a rifle shot and the next thing I knew Bruce was staggering back toward me." My voice was clear. I had control of myself now.

"You didn't see anyone?"

I shook my head.

"What about any animals, birds? Things like that."

I saw what Geoff was trying to do. He wanted to make it into a hunting accident. "I didn't see anything. I was too shocked to notice."

"Where did the shot come from?"

"Over across there somewhere, I guess," I pointed vaguely across the creek. Geoff started to say something else but stopped as we heard the sound of a car door slamming and King's voice calling. "Geoff. Where are you?"

Geoff ran back up the slight incline to the road and reappeared a moment later with King and Don Mason. Geoff was shaking his head, "There's nothing you can do, Don. He's dead."

"My God," I heard King whisper when he saw Bruce. He knelt beside the body, rocking slightly back and forth, his elbows on his knees, his head in his hands. I could only wonder what he was thinking.

Geoff and Don Mason put the body on a stretcher and carried it out to the road. I heard a motor start up and then the crunching sounds of tires. Geoff came back. He went over to King, bent down and spoke to him quietly. Not wanting to intrude, I wandered down to the creek. How utterly cruel life was, I protested, and then corrected myself. It wasn't life that was to blame, it was people.

King was standing now, stoop shouldered, looking suddenly very old. Slowly, he squared his shoulders and I heard him say to Geoff, "We'd better go. I'll have to break it to Elizabeth." He walked heavily toward the road.

Geoff stood looking at me. "Coming, Jenny?"

I sighed. Then I remembered the mare. I would have to ride her back to the stables. It was just as well. I didn't particularly want to be present when the news was broken to the rest of the Cabots. I wondered how they would take it. "There's the mare," I reminded Geoff. "I'll ride her back."

I waited until I heard his jeep leave and then went up to the road to get the mare. I mounted and turned her back toward the creek, carefully picking my way across to the other side. I headed for the area where the shot had come from—a line of trees that ran along the bottom of the cliff. The killer would have had to stand among them in order to get both shelter and a clear shot. It didn't take me long to find the faint heel marks of cowboy boots and the spent cartridge. A few seconds later, shoved in between a tumbled mass of rocks, I found the rifle. I carefully pulled it out and held it cradled in my hands. The exquisite hand-carved stock was unmistakable. I had seen it before —in the rifle rack in the Colvada mill office.

———◆———

When I finally got back to the Castle, Don Mason's dilapidated, old station wagon was parked in the driveway. I stood, looking at the big, heavy front door and tried to gather myself for the scene I knew was occurring inside. Reluctantly, I went in. They were all in the library. Elizabeth, her face contorted into an ugly unrecognizable mask, was screaming hysterically at Geoff. "You! You killed him! The way you have everything else. Murderer!" Geoff stood, teeth clenched, staring back at her, saying nothing. His face was ashen beneath its tan. King was attempting to comfort Elizabeth, but was having little success. She kept screaming accusations at Geoff. Lynn, looking grimmer than I had ever seen her, turned to Don Mason, who was nervously shifting from one foot to the other.

"You'd better give her a sedative," Lynn told him coolly. "You realize of course that she's beside herself. She doesn't know what she's saying." I marveled at Lynn's command. Somehow I had expected her to be the one to break down, not Elizabeth. Carole sat in one of the big chairs, her head bowed, for once saying nothing. I felt like an interloper. I was sure Don Mason felt the same way. The Cabots had closed in around themselves and it wasn't a place for outsiders.

Distinctly uncomfortable, I went over to Lynn and asked if there was anything I could do. "No," she answered without looking at me. "You've done quite enough already." Her tone was so devoid of emphasis that I couldn't tell how she meant her comment to be taken. I turned to leave the room. "On second thought," she said, "you could take Christopher out of here. This is no place for him."

For the first time I saw Christopher, huddled in a corner, half hidden by the couch. I held out my hand to him and we left. We went down to the stables where I curried and groomed the bay and the mare. Chris helped me for a while. His face was serious as though he was pondering something. "Jenny," he said suddenly, "why does Grandmother think that my father killed Uncle Bruce?" So, I thought despairingly, he had believed Elizabeth's ravings.

I tried to smooth it over. "Your grandmother is very upset. She loved your Uncle Bruce very much. She's not herself. She just needed to yell at someone. That's all." It sounded lame. I didn't buy it, why should he. Elizabeth had meant every word. I suddenly wondered if that was why Geoff had reacted so each time I'd thought he might be responsible for the attacks on Christopher and me. I'd once thought fleetingly that Elizabeth might have blamed Geoff for Philip Cabot's death. I had discarded the idea as absurd. He had only been five. Now, I wasn't so sure. It would explain a number of things.

"Do you think he did it?" Christopher asked me for the second time.

I brought my attention back to him. "No. Of course not." Finally, I could be certain that Geoff was innocent. He wouldn't have had time to kill Bruce, ride down the creek and be at the mill by the time I got there. No, the killer was not Geoff. It was someone else with ready access to the mill office.

◆

Dinner was a quiet affair. We ate in the kitchen—Lynn, Geoff, Chris and I. Afterward, Lynn and I did the dishes, but neither of us spoke, each lost in our own thoughts. The Castle was oppressive and I soon escaped, walking down to Mithral Falls. Was it only last night, I thought, that Elizabeth had brought me here to warn me about Geoff? The pace of events had left me with a feeling of unreality about everything that had gone on before Bruce's death. The picture of him, lying on the ground, his life seeping away kept flashing before me. There was no reason for him to die, except that he had been with me in the wrong place at the wrong time. It was my fault. From the beginning it had been my fault. Lynn was right. I had done more than enough. I had come in, brashly asking questions, scraping raw old wounds, tearing open old scars. I was no match for the violence that throbbed in the veins of this family and yet now, even if I had wanted to, I knew that I couldn't extricate myself from the web of their lives.

Geoff found me sitting on a rock trying to decide what I should do now. He sat beside me and looked at me with his strangely disturbing, unfathomable eyes. "How are you doing?" he asked finally.

"All right."

"That must have been pretty awful for you."

I wondered what he was after. "Yes. It was."

He sat quietly for a while, eyes downcast, tracing a pattern on the rock. I waited for him to continue. When he didn't, I prodded gently. "What did you want, Geoff?"

The long lashes swept up suddenly and my heart jolted. "I realize that whoever fired that shot was trying to kill you and not Bruce." He paused. "I'm not the one responsible. Elizabeth has hated me all my life because she thinks I somehow was responsible for setting off the explosion that killed my father. She's never forgiven me for being there when it happened. She even managed to convince Nancy that I'd done it. Nancy was so naïve. That was one of the reasons I married her—she didn't know the meaning of unhappiness and loneliness. I'm afraid we taught her that and more. She had no chance in this family. Then when I caused her miscarriage, Elizabeth really had a weapon. I don't know what you think of me, Jenny, but I'm no killer. You've got to believe that."

I knew my eyes were bright with tears. I reached out and touched his hand. "I know you're not." I stopped there, knowing that I didn't dare continue without revealing how I felt about him.

Picking up my hand, he turned it over and ran his finger along the lines in my palm. "Clearly, it's not very safe for you around here. I want you to leave. Go back to San Francisco. I want you to take Christopher with you. I know he'll be safe with you. When we get to the bottom of things, I'll let you know."

I withdrew my hand. "No, Geoff. I can't leave. I'm not running this time."

"That's final? There's no way I can talk you out of it?"

"None. I'm sorry."

"I was afraid of that." He reached in his shirt pocket and drew out a key. "Here, then. This is the key to your door. Would you at least keep Chris with you at night and make sure you keep the door locked?"

I clutched the key in my hand. Thank God, I thought over and over. Thank God, it's not Geoff.

CHAPTER 11

Castle Cabot took on an ominous air. Bruce's death seemed to hang over it like a palpable fog, coloring everything. Everyone retreated into his own shell and remained there. We seldom spoke to each other, and certainly no one mentioned Bruce or the shooting. Geoff spent most of his time at the mines. Elizabeth remained in bed, heavily sedated for three days. Then, with Don Mason hovering nervously in the background, she came downstairs for the funeral. It was a small affair, with only the members of the family, plus Paul and myself. As soon as it was over, she went back upstairs, locked herself in her room and refused to come out.

Lynn, maintaining her marvelous stoic calm, took over running the Castle and, being the only one who could get her to respond, looked after Elizabeth. King remained grim throughout. He made a few initial attempts to comfort Elizabeth, but she rejected them. Carole kept to herself until after the funeral. Then, to everyone's surprise, she announced that she was going to leave. There was nothing for her in Kingsville, she said, and she was going to go somewhere and start over again. In two days she was gone. Paul told me that King had made her a handsome settlement. She had the money now, but somehow I wondered if that would be enough. For all her bitchiness, I began to think that Carole had really cared for Bruce.

There were only six of us left now. Seven, if one counted Christopher. The question that continued to haunt me was when would the killer strike again? I spent most of that week trying to stay away from the Castle, keeping Christopher with me as much as possible, attempting to shield him from the gloomy pall. I had told no one about the gun I'd found, and given King's word that the whole thing had been some bizarre accident—a hunter who was a very poor shot or something of that sort—the county sheriff had agreed to conveniently forget the matter. I couldn't help but think of Sarah Gibson's dark hints about the Cabots. "If King Cabot says it's an accident," she had remarked when talking about my father. I had to admit that she was right.

I bided my time, knowing that the killer would come after me again. It was only a matter of waiting. This time, however, I would be prepared for him.

I went to the library one afternoon, fixed myself a martini and sat staring at the paneled entrance to the Stair. Somehow I always came back to the Stair. It was well kept up. That lock had been new. The panel motor worked smoothly. Only one person could have kept the Stair in use for all these years, and that was Kingston. Lynn had no capability for maintaining the Stair, nor did Elizabeth. Moreover, Lynn had no motive for murdering my father. It had to be Kingston. Everything added up. Until I came to Christopher that is. He was the stumbling block. Why would King make him the eventual heir and then try to kill him? A blind, perhaps. The perfect alibi. But even so, I reasoned, why would he want to kill him?

My mind sorted through one improbable scenario after another. It had to go back to Philip Cabot. Perhaps, I thought, I had been working from the wrong assumptions. All along I'd assumed that my father had killed Philip in order to free my mother from Kingston, and that years later one of the Cabots had found out about it and had arranged his "disappearance." Suppose, though, that he hadn't killed Philip, but merely knew who had? Perhaps instead of there being two murderers—my father and the present killer—there was really only one. Who else could have wanted Philip Cabot dead?

I sipped my martini speculatively. And then, suddenly, I had it. I saw at last what I had been overlooking.

Going up to my room and extracting the now-important key

from my purse, I changed into a long-sleeved shirt. It would be chilly underground, so for good measure I tossed my wind-breaker over my arm. Downstairs in Kingston's office, I found a hard hat and a miner's lamp. I was going to be prepared this time. Deftly, I hooked the battery on my belt, slid the lamp into its slot on the front of the hat and slipped into the library. I meant to go onto the Stair. I was sure that somewhere near the exit to Rob Roy Basin I would find the killer's black garb and Christopher's saddle. I would need them when I confronted the Cabots. I checked Paul's map and started toward the bookcase. Then I decided that I wanted a little assurance. Picking up the phone, I called Angus.

"In two hours, if you haven't heard from me, call Geoff and Paul and tell them I've gone on the Mithral Stair."

"You can't go on the Stair," Angus protested. "That's sui-cide."

Maybe, I thought, but not in the way you mean, Angus. And at any rate, I had to chance it. There was no other way. With luck it would all be over in a few hours.

I pulled the *Flying Dutchman* from the shelf, popped open the covering hiding the buttons and pressed the top one. Slowly, the panel moved. While it was opening, I replaced the books, camouflaging the entrance mechanism once again. Glancing hastily behind me, I stepped through the panel. Turning the lamp on, I flashed it around, looking for the buttons on this side that would close the door. There would be no reason for them to be hidden—not on the inside. After a brief search I found them, pressed one experimentally and, when it didn't work, pressed the other. The panel began to close. Satisfied, I went down the steps and along the tunnel to the door. I inserted the key confidently in the padlock. A turn of my wrist and the lock fell off in my hands. I put my shoulder to the heavy door and nudged it open. Now, at last, I was on the Mithral Stair.

Immediately, a cold, damp blast of air hit me and the smell of wet earth filled my nostrils. A wave of fear passed through me, but resolutely, I ignored it. What I had to do was too important to let my fear of the underground get the best of me. The rock walls of the tunnel glistened dully in the small circle of my lamp. There were several pools of water standing on the tunnel floor. Revolving the light slowly, I took a careful look at the timbers propping up the tunnel. I had been right. There was no sign of rot. Cautiously, I proceeded.

After several thousand feet, an iron grating barred the passageway. Immediately before it another tunnel forked off to the left. At least, I thought, it saves making decisions. Another few hundred feet and I came to a ladder, propped up against the side of the tunnel. Flicking the light upward I saw the hole in the tunnel ceiling. This would be one of the raises taking me from one level of the Stair to another. With growing excitement, I tested the ladder, found that it was sturdy and climbed up. This new tunnel ran perpendicular to the one below, driving back into the very roots of Mithral Mountain. It was somewhat drier.

I moved along the tunnel, stopping often to inspect side tunnels which shot off this main artery. Sometimes they were partially filled with rubble; other times they were dead ends. At length I came to the second ladder. I examined it closely. It wasn't in as good a condition as the first ladder but it looked safe. Carefully, I mounted it to the third level of the Mithral Stair—the ill-fated Grubstake tunnel.

The tunnel headed off to the right, slanting uphill slightly. I walked for about ten minutes, looking eagerly for the raise that would take me to the next level. Instead, I rounded a sharp corner and stopped short as my light picked up the huge, tumbled mass of broken rock that marked Philip Cabot's grave.

"Damn," I muttered softly. Paul's map had shown another part of the Stair on the Grubstake tunnel. Apparently it was either beyond the obstruction ahead of me or else had been brought down in the cave-in. I looked once more at the wall of broken rock. I didn't wonder that they had never dug Philip out. The fractured, blasted pile seemed to stretch interminably into the blackness. I could see the tunnel above, but my light wasn't strong enough to illuminate more than the narrow space between the top of the mound of debris and the curved roof. I would have to go back to the second level. The connections of the Stair which led to Rob Roy Basin must lead from there. Paul's map didn't show them, but I had no idea when it had been drawn. The raises could have been made at a later date.

As I moved my light, I saw the skeleton. It lay at the base of the rock pile, half clothed in disintegrating cloth. Instinctively, I recoiled and my heart began hammering uncertainly. I forced myself to take a closer look. Every white bone was in place. No one had disturbed them for three years. Gingerly, I reached out and turned the brightly grinning skull. A small round hole in the cranium silently proclaimed how my father had met his death.

I had no doubt it was my father. When, a moment later, I found the tarnished gold band he had always worn, I had positive proof. It was no wonder they had never found him, even with the bloodhounds. All the time he had been lying here—on the Mithral Stair.

I flashed my light along the skeleton. My eye caught a piece of paper. It was an old cigarette pack. I fingered it while I stared at my father's remains. I had come to Kingsville pricked by curiosity and memories. I had found a trail of murder and deceit that stretched through two generations. Idly, I put my fingers inside the cigarette pack. Instantly, I was alert. There was something inside. Puzzled, I pulled out three folded sheets of paper covered with my father's large handwriting, faded now with time. "I rigged the explosion that killed Philip Cabot," it began.

I read through it twice. Sitting on my heels, I refolded the papers and stuffed them in my back pocket. I wouldn't need the clothes and saddle now. I had finally found my way out of the maze. I could go back to the Castle and face the Cabots with the truth.

Sharp pieces of flying rock jabbed into my cheek and I jumped. My hand flew up to my face and I could feel a few drops of blood. Then I heard the low, triumphant laugh. The same as before, only this time I knew who it was. In fact, I realized, I had half been expecting her.

"Jenny," the familiar voice called. "Are you there? I didn't hit you did I? I didn't mean to. Not yet. I want you to sweat it out awhile first. The way I have these past weeks while you've been poking your fingers into everything. Your father tried to make me sweat it out too. You're such fools, both of you." The voice taunted me. For the first time in my life I wanted to kill someone. Amazed at the naked wave of anger, I clamped a tight control on myself. I needed to be especially cool now. I was fighting for my life.

Quickly, I switched off my lamp and moved silently to the other side of the tunnel so that I was protected by the slight curve of the wall. "You'll never get away with it, Elizabeth," I warned.

Again the laugh. "You think not. There's no one to stop me. You certainly can't."

"I wasn't foolish enough to come up here without telling someone where I was going. If I'm not back in an hour, Paul and Geoff will be up here looking for me."

"Geoff." She spat the word out. "I tried to warn you, but you wouldn't listen. You wouldn't leave. You kept digging into things that weren't your business. You," her voice rose and became ugly "had to fall for Geoff." The hideous chuckle echoed through the tunnel. I found myself thinking that she had gone mad; that Bruce's death had unhinged her mind. Then she spoke again, and this time she was in control. "You've backed yourself into this corner, Jenny. Surely you can see that I've no alternative. I don't want to do this." Her voice was pleading, cajoling now as though she were trying to win me over to her side. "I have to kill you now."

"No one's going to be killed," I asserted far more firmly than I felt. "I told you. Paul and Geoff will be here shortly."

"No they won't," she countered smugly. "I took the precaution of disconnecting the starter on the motor that opens the panel. You're not smart enough to outwit me, Jenifer."

My heart sank. I had no doubt that she was telling the truth. There was no possibility of rescue. They couldn't get here soon enough. Why, I asked myself savagely, hadn't I told Lynn what I was doing?

"It still won't work, Elizabeth," I continued to challenge her.

"Even if you kill me, Lynn knows what you are, and she won't stand by this time."

"Lynn," she scoffed. "She'll never do anything. She loves Kingston too much. She knows what it would do to him to find out."

"Don't count on that."

She laughed. "Getting desperate, aren't you, Jenny? Just like your father. He was a weak man. Putty in my hands. He loved your mother so much that he'd do anything to get her, even kill Philip. The fool." I could hear the contempt dripping from her voice.

"And when he decided he couldn't live with himself any longer and was going to tell King the truth, you killed him. You got him to come up here and killed him. You've certainly made good use of the Stair, I'll say that. You could come and go from the Castle as you pleased and no one was the wiser. That's how you got Christopher's saddle out of sight, how you managed to escape so quickly when you tried to push me over the Falls, how you managed to get over into Cottonwood the day you shot Bruce."

I was answered by the sting of splintered rock. There was no sound in the tunnel and I realized belatedly that she had a silencer on the gun. That way there was no risk of causing a cave-in—until she was ready to bury me. It seemed she thought of everything.

"So you figured it all out, did you?" she taunted.

"Most of it. How did you get my father up here, anyway?" I was stalling for time.

Elizabeth seemed disposed to talk. "He'd come down the Stair from Mithral Basin hoping to find Kingston alone so he could 'confess.' I had no idea that the two of them had maintained the Stair after Philip died. I was in the library when he came out. I got him to tell me what he was going to do. I tried to talk him out of it, but he was determined." She chuckled. "He tried to reassure me that he wasn't going to reveal my part in Philip's accident. He was going to take the whole blame. I knew better than to trust him. King always kept a revolver in the desk drawer. I pulled it out and tried to frighten John into being silent. He ran for the Stair. I followed him. He thought he could evade me by coming up here, but he wasn't clever enough to outwit me. As I followed him, I realized I had to kill him. It was simple.

"After that, I explored the Stair and found the parts that King and John had kept up. I decided I could use it in emergencies. I never had to until King changed the will. Then I had to strike out against Christopher. I couldn't let Geoff's son inherit everything I'd worked to get for myself and for Bruce.

"And then you came, sticking your nose into everything, asking questions. Little Miss Detective! When I overheard you tell Lynn you'd found out about the Mithral Stair I tried to scare you off, but you wouldn't mind your own business. And on top of everything else, you had to fall for Geoff." She spat out his name, the hatred evident in her voice.

I didn't say anything. I was thinking frantically. I knew that my only hope lay in getting to the Jackpot tunnel on the fifth level of the Stair and escaping into Rob Roy Basin. I was sure now that the second-level tunnel was the route that had been maintained, but Elizabeth stood between me and that escape route. Remembering Paul's map, I thought that if I could reach the fourth level somehow, I could find my way out. I would have to scramble up the pile of rocks and inch my way through the narrow opening at the top. From there luck would have to see me through. I wasn't sure that portion of the fourth level had been kept up. I didn't particularly like choosing between Elizabeth and an abandoned tunnel, but there was nothing I could do about it. The first problem was how to keep Elizabeth from realizing what I was doing. She expected me to give in, to offer little resistance—like my father. My jaw set determinedly. Keep her talking, I thought. It was the only thing I could do.

"I still don't understand why you hate Geoff so." I tossed the topic out.

"Geoff." She was scornful. "It's very simple. Philip lied to me you see. He told me he was the Cabot heir, that he had the money. That was why I married him. It was too late when I discovered the truth."

Slowly, inch by inch as she talked, I edged my way up the mound of rocks, reaching for handholds in the dark, holding my breath for fear any noise would reveal what I was doing.

"I went after King and he fell in love with me, but Philip wouldn't give me a divorce. He tried everything to get me back. He used Geoff against me. We were a family, he said. Because of Geoff, Kingston wouldn't do anything. He was so honorable about it! He wouldn't even touch me while I was his brother's wife. Nothing would move either of them. Five years of hell we lived through before I realized that I could talk John into making Philip's death look like an accident. I knew that if I was free, King would marry me and then John could have your mother. I had tender sensibilities in those days. I didn't want to do it myself. I'm not such a milquetoast now. Geoff has been a constant reminder of Philip, of those five years, of what I was forced to do. It wouldn't have been necessary if he had just given way. And he might have if it hadn't been for Geoff. Of course I hated him."

It was the typical twisted psychology. Always the blame lay with others. How many years she had fooled everyone. Everyone but Lynn. Elizabeth was right, Lynn adored King, but she admired and loved her mother as well. No wonder it had torn her apart. Elizabeth was a consummate actress. I'd believed her implicitly until I'd suddenly realized that I'd always assumed that she and Philip had been happily married. Once I threw that assumption out, Elizabeth was the only person with a motive for killing Philip, my father, Christopher and myself. Money. It all came down to the Cabot wealth.

Elizabeth kept talking, railing against Geoff, scornfully describing how she had encouraged Nancy and Bruce, blaming me for intruding, for Bruce's death. I listened, realizing that she was telling me so much because she didn't expect me to live to repeat it. While she talked, I crept closer to the fourth level of the Mithral Stair.

Then what I dreaded happened. My foot slipped on a rock and it went tumbling down, the sound echoing in the tunnel. That would bring Elizabeth running. There was no need for caution now. I snapped my light on for a second, memorized the rock pile above me, then in darkness once again, straightened and scrambled up the remaining distance to the top, heedless of the miniature landslide I was causing. I heard her muttered exclamation, just as I reached the top. Deliberately I kicked at a rather large, jagged piece of rock and sent it plunging down toward her. Then I began wriggling along the narrow space between the ceiling of the fourth level and the tumbled mass that formed Philip Cabot's tomb. As I did so I again felt the flying splinters of rock, and this time I heard the whine of the bullet as it passed by me. Heart thudding wildly, fighting down panic, I redoubled my efforts. I had at most about ten minutes before she could climb the rock pile and I would be within her gun sights. I knew I had to make the most of it.

The cave-in was almost at an end. Another few hundred feet and the rock pile began sloping downward. Again I scrambled down the slope not caring how many rocks I dislodged, nor how much noise I made. There would be time for silence later. Once on solid ground, I quickly turned on my light and flashed it around the tunnel. It was in better shape than I had expected, mostly due to the dryness of the rock. Two broken timbers hung from the roof and piles of rock dotted the floor and sides of the tunnel. Not that it mattered. I was committed. I ran headlong down the narrow passageway, casting quick glances back over my shoulder, looking for the first glimpse of Elizabeth's lamp, praying that there would be a curve in the tunnel so that I would be out of sight. I skirted a black hole in the tunnel floor that marked the raise coming up from the cut off Grubstake tunnel. I dared not take it. Elizabeth had dismantled the door. To go back down the Stair would be to trap myself.

I counted off eight minutes as I ran and then I turned my lamp off. I didn't want to make a sitting target. Hugging the right-hand wall, my hand out in front of me, feeling for obstructions, I moved, step by step now, farther away from help and deeper into the heart of the mountain.

I passed by tunnel openings that I dared not take time to investigate. Guiding myself by a combination of panic, instinct and a memory of Paul's map, I thought that I would soon come to another ladder which would take me to the fifth level—the level of the Jackpot tunnel. How was I going to see the ladder in the dark I didn't know. I knew that I was gaining a little time for as Elizabeth came to each of the side tunnels she would have to pause to make sure I hadn't detoured or tried to hide and then escape behind her. I was breathing hard now and, despite the chill damp of the underground, I was bathed in perspiration. I could feel the hot, salty drops running down my cheeks.

Looking back I couldn't see Elizabeth's light. Was she merely waiting for me to fall into a trap, I wondered, or had she really disappeared somewhere for a moment? Knowing that I desperately needed to have a look at my surroundings, I removed the battery from my belt, took the lamp and carefully set it over on the opposite side of the tunnel, making sure the lamp was facing downward. I turned the knob to activate it and leaped back, flattening myself against the wall. Nothing happened. The lamp made a faint, small orange circle on the ground. Gently, I pulled at the battery with my foot until the lamp turned over and the tunnel ahead of me was flooded briefly with light. Instantly, there was a crackling sound of glass breaking and the light went out. Elizabeth *had* been waiting. Playing cat and mouse with me. My horror at her calculated villainy was matched only by my fear for my own life.

The glimpse ahead had been enough. At the farthest perimeter of the light I had seen the dark shape of the next ladder. Leaving the defunct lamp, I rushed toward it. Hands outstretched I bumped into the ladder and stifled the impulse to exclaim aloud at the pain which shot through my knee. Rapidly, I climbed to the fifth level. I tried to pull the ladder up after me, or at least fling it down to the tunnel below, but it wouldn't move. I abandoned that effort and returned to the task of finding my way as rapidly as possible in the blackness. My hands were cut and bruised from the rough rock on the tunnel wall, but I hardly noticed for I could see Elizabeth's lamp bobbing in the darkness behind me. I stumbled over piles of rocks on the floor of the tunnel and occasionally stubbed my toes against errant

rail ties that had been flung to the side of the passageway. I had
to stay within reach of the walls. If not, I knew I could lose my
sense of balance. After what seemed like an eternity I came to a
wide opening forking off to the right. I plunged into it. This had
to be the Jackpot. If it weren't . . . . I couldn't let myself com-
plete that thought.

Elizabeth had made up a lot of ground. I could hear her
steady, ominous footsteps now and then suddenly the beam of
her lamp casting shadows in front of me. This is it, I whispered
to myself. A split second later the shadows faded and I was
again in darkness. Of course, I thought, she had a rifle so she
would have to stop to fire and, when she did, I would move out
of her range. I decided to run as best as I could, keeping my
hand on the side of the tunnel. I could hear her footsteps quicken
as she too picked up her pace. Then the hammering pulse in my
ears drowned out all the other sounds.

Hurtling around a corner, I stopped short. Ahead I could see
blue sky framed by the black sides of the tunnel adit. I ran full
speed toward it, lurching from side to side now so I wouldn't
present a good target.

I gained it none too soon. Elizabeth had stopped once I was
silhouetted in the light from the opening and had started firing.
Splinters of rock rained on me as I leaped out of the opening
and bounded down the slope toward the road that led back to
the Castle. I squinted at the bright sunshine; the warm air hit me
like a blanket. A spurt of dust and rocks to my left reminded me
that I hadn't escaped her yet. By the time I reached Rob Roy
Creek her shots were getting closer. My immediate impulse was
to seek cover. Without thinking what I was doing, I spotted a
large boulder and dropped down behind it. Two bullets spanged
off the top of the boulder. Then I realized that I had trapped myself. As long as I had been moving, I'd had a chance. Now I was
pinned down. I couldn't move because as soon as I did I would be
dead. And if I stayed here, the result would be the same. I went
limp with exhaustion and fear. I heard Elizabeth chuckling and
a flame of anger flooded over me, only to be followed by a wave
of despair. Dead end, Jenny, I told myself. A literal dead end.

Cautiously, I peered out from behind the boulder trying to locate Elizabeth. I saw her then for the first time since my nightmare had begun. Her auburn hair streaming out behind her, dressed in jeans and a loose-fitting shirt, she was edging her way between me and the top of the falls, effectively cutting off my access to the road. As soon as my head appeared, I saw the rifle swing to her shoulder and I ducked back under cover. The bullet struck where my head had been, spraying me with chips of rock. There was no escape. I leaned against the boulder waiting for what I knew was coming. Surprisingly, I was calm now.

Then I heard the whining sound of a jeep and over it, cool and unwavering, King's voice. "That's far enough, Elizabeth," he said. "Put the gun down."

The jeep stopped. I strained, waiting for Elizabeth's reply, but there was only silence. Then, a choked cry. Slowly, I stood up, half-leaning against the boulder that I had used as a refuge. I could see the long tubular scars left by the bullets. Kingston was at the top of the Falls, his head down, his shoulders slumped, shaking convulsively. Lynn was with him. I couldn't see Elizabeth.

Suddenly, Geoff was beside me. He caught me in his arms and kissed me almost breathlessly. "Jenny. Jenny," he muttered. "You crazy little fool." He crushed me to him, running his hands over me as if to make sure I was all right. I clung to him, closing my eyes and letting reality seep back into my consciousness.

"It's all right now, darling. It's all over," he kept reassuring me. "You're safe now."

"Elizabeth?" I asked, my voice muffled against his shoulder.

I could feel him tense and then relax. "She threw herself over the Falls. I don't see how she could survive." He spoke softly, almost sadly.

I sighed. So many lives truncated; so many others nearly ruined. For a fistful of gold or silver, for a large bank account and social standing. Such a terrible waste.

I stepped away from Geoff and smiled tremulously up at him. "I'm all right," I told him. "Really."

He returned my smile and my heart began thudding—a slow,

sure, confident pulse. Life returning. "You little fire-eater." He ran his forefinger along my brow and down the side of my face, brushing my hair back away from my cheek. Then he bent his head and kissed me, slowly, gently. When he finished, he put his arm around my shoulders and we walked toward the Falls. Lynn and King were still standing together. Paul came down the slope from the tunnel and joined us.

"Jenny," Geoff said at last. "I want you to go down to the Castle with Lynn. She's going to need to have someone around. Paul, King and I will get Elizabeth's body. Will you do that for me?"

Mutely, I nodded.

Geoff released me and I stood with Paul while he went over to Lynn. She turned to face him and I saw that her face was ashen, almost ghostly, her eyes shadowed with pain. "Why don't both you and Jenny go down to the Castle," Geoff suggested to her. "You'd better call Don about the coroner. The rest of us will get Elizabeth."

She stared at him blankly. She was, I thought, close to a breakdown. "We're all here if you need us, Lynn," he said gently. Her eyes filled suddenly and tears spilled down her cheeks. Geoff pulled her to him and she held onto him.

I looked quickly at Paul, wondering what he was thinking. He was staring at the three Cabots. I put my hand on his arm. "Paul."

"It's going to take her a long time to come out of this," he said, not taking his eyes from Lynn.

"She's going to need you more than ever," I told him.

He looked at me then. "Elizabeth. I just can't believe it. When you told me that wild idea of yours, Elizabeth was the last person I would have thought of." He shook his head in bewilderment.

"How did you find us?" I asked.

"Angus. He was disturbed after you called him, so he stewed for an hour and then he came to see me. Lynn was in my office and when she heard what you were doing, she bolted back to the Castle. I followed her. Elizabeth was gone and one of the rifles was missing from the office. We tried the panel and when it wouldn't open, we got Geoff and King. Lynn told us the whole thing then. We broke down the panel and Geoff and I came through the tunnels trying to find you. King knew this exit had never been dynamited, so he and Lynn came up here in case you managed to find your way out. Geoff and I did find Christopher's saddle and the clothes Elizabeth used, but the two of you were too far ahead for us to catch up. We came out of the tunnels just as Elizabeth threw herself over the Falls. I don't know how you did it, Jenny. Especially without a light most of the way. Those tunnels are treacherous."

"You do what you have to," I said softly.

———◆———

Lynn and I went down to the Castle. She moved in a daze. Woodenly, she called Don Mason and asked him to arrange for the undertaker. While she was doing that I found Christopher, told him briefly that his grandmother was dead, and, deciding that it would be best if he weren't subjected to the scene that was sure to come, called Angus and, explaining quickly what had happened, asked if he would take the boy to the hotel for a few hours. Angus agreed, and when I had bundled Christopher and Strider into his jeep I turned my attention to Lynn.

She had retreated into the library and sat in one of the big, stuffed arm chairs, staring vacantly at the oak bookcase that had covered the panel opening to the Mithral Stair. It had been hacked to pieces. Two axes leaned against the big desk, and books from the shelves were strewn on the floor. The damp, earthy smell of the tunnel had seeped into the room.

I knelt down beside Lynn and put my hand over hers. "Lynn." I didn't know what else to say.

She looked at me, her brown eyes filled with pain. "I almost got you killed." She said it flatly, with no emphasis.

"It wasn't your fault. You did what you thought you had to. Do you want to talk about it?"

It was a long time before she replied. When she did begin to speak, it was in a low monotone and I had to strain to catch her

words. "The day he disappeared, I overheard your father arguing with Elizabeth. Something about Philip. I couldn't understand all of it. Later that day, quite by accident, I saw Elizabeth
coming out of the panel. She had a gun—a revolver—in her
hand and she seemed very pleased about something. I hadn't
known about the Stair until then. When your father turned up
missing and the search parties couldn't find him, I began to suspect what had happened. I couldn't believe it, but I couldn't escape the conclusion either. I tried to explore the Stair, but
couldn't get past the locked door.

"I confronted Elizabeth with what I knew. She laughed and
told me about the Stair and said that she sometimes went to
Philip's tomb. She took the gun because there were rats in the
tunnels and she was afraid of them. It sounded reasonable, but I
wasn't sure. I'd been uneasy over the way she'd acted during the
whole mess with Nancy.

"You asked me about Nancy once, and I didn't tell you much
because I was afraid it would tip you off about Elizabeth. Nancy
was a shy, sweet girl. Insecure. She wasn't strong. I think that's
why Geoff married her. Because she wasn't like any of us. Anyway, Elizabeth couldn't stand it. She'd always hated Geoff. She
didn't want him to be happy. Then when Chris was born it was
worse because she knew he would be the Cabot heir if Bruce and
Carole didn't have children. She tried to drive them apart. I've
always suspected that she put Carole up to going after Geoff.
Nancy was bewildered. She was no match for Carole. She accused Geoff of being unfaithful to her. He went into one of his
moods and didn't talk to anyone for days. Bruce was hanging
around and saw that he had an easy pigeon in Nancy. He was
everything Geoff wasn't—romantic, charming, gay. Nancy fell
for him. Geoff went back into his shell. Elizabeth kept working
on Nancy, telling her stories about Geoff. She had her believing
that at five Geoff was responsible for Philip's accident. It went
from bad to worse. Elizabeth was very subtle about it, but she
stuck the knife into Geoff and Nancy's marriage every chance
she got. She half-convinced Geoff that Christopher was Bruce's,
hoping that Geoff would shut him out too.

"I never realized what was happening until just before Nancy left. She was bitter that King made her leave Christopher behind so she came to me, hoping that if I knew the whole story, I'd intercede with King. I tried, but he wasn't about to change his mind.

"Anyway, when I began to suspect Elizabeth being in on your father's disappearance and I knew they'd been arguing about Philip, I remembered what Nancy had told me. I'd always known that Elizabeth didn't like Geoff, but I began to realize that she'd hated Philip and she hated Geoff as well. I started to worry about what she might do, so I decided to watch her, to try to keep her from harming anyone else.

"That was three years ago. I could never marry Paul because I would have to leave the Castle, and I couldn't let him come to live here because I knew he'd find out about Elizabeth and go to the authorities. I could never go to King—I had no proof, nothing solid. I knew that only some tangible piece of evidence would convince him. He'd stop her then, but it would destroy him. I thought I could put myself between Elizabeth and Geoff and no one would ever need to know. When King decided to force Bruce and Carole to have children and changed the will, the attacks on Christopher started. I was sure about Elizabeth then. She'd go to any length to keep Geoff's son from inheriting the money.

"Even then I couldn't say anything. I tried to convince King to change the will back to Bruce, but he wouldn't. I went to Elizabeth again and told her I knew what she was doing. She just laughed at me. All I could do then was try to protect Christopher. Even after Bruce, I kept quiet. I felt certain that that mistake would stop her, but it made her more determined to kill you. It's my fault," Lynn finished, her head down. "All of it. If I'd gone to King in the beginning, none of it would have happened. Bruce would still be alive. And Elizabeth."

"You can't blame yourself, Lynn. As you say, King wouldn't have believed you before. It's over now. You've got to go on. King will need you. And there's Paul."

She smiled faintly. That sardonic Cabot smile. "You're very generous, Jenny. I wish it were that simple."

There were so many more things I wanted to talk about, but they would all have to wait. We had gone far enough for now. I stood up and, skirting the books littering the floor, went over to the bar and fixed both of us a stiff drink. We sat in silence and waited for the men to come with Elizabeth's body.

They brought her into the dining room.

I thought Lynn was going to break down when she looked at her mother's battered lifeless form, but she got control of herself and turned her attention to Kingston. He was in a state of shock. He couldn't be moved from his position beside the body. Lynn tried to comfort him. Geoff stood by awkwardly. Paul and I stayed in a corner of the room.

Suddenly, King turned to us and spoke in an anguished, grief-filled voice. "Why? Why did she do it?"

I could answer his question now. Before I would have had shrewd guesses, but after listening to Elizabeth in the tunnel and reading my father's written "confession" I at last knew the whole story.

"For the money," I said quietly.

Geoff leaned against the mantel, his head propped against his fist. "You may as well tell us everything now, Jenny. We'll have to hear it sooner or later."

I looked at King and then at Lynn. "Are you sure it's wise to go into it now?"

King sat down heavily in one of the caned dining room chairs. "Yes," he said. "I want to hear it. Go ahead, Jenny."

"All right. I'll try to make it as coherent as I can. When I went onto the Stair this afternoon, I'd guessed a lot of it. Then I found a 'confession' my father had written for you, King, stuffed in a cigarette pack by his body, and that confirmed most of my guesses. Elizabeth talked quite a bit—before we began our chase through the Stair—and filled in the rest of the gaps."

King reacted slowly, interrupting me with a hoarse voice. "John's body is on the Stair?"

"Yes. At the foot of the cave-in in the Grubstake tunnel. Elizabeth shot him."

King looked at the floor and put his hand over his eyes. "Oh, my God," he whispered, more to himself than to anyone else.

I paused, uncertain about whether to continue. I met Lynn's eyes.

"Go on, Jenny," she said. "You may as well start at the beginning."

I took a long breath and then plunged in. "It goes back to when Philip and Elizabeth were married. He was mad about her and he knew she wouldn't marry him unless he was rich, so he told her he was the Cabot heir. When she came to Kingsville and discovered he'd lied, she turned on him. She felt betrayed. She encouraged King to fall in love with her intending to divorce Philip and marry the real heir, only she hadn't counted on King's loyalty to his brother, nor on Philip's stubbornness. He used Geoff as a tool to keep her with him. She began to hate them both for keeping her from what she wanted.

"In the meantime my mother had come to Kingsville and had gotten interested in King. Since Elizabeth wasn't free, King decided he might as well marry her, which would have been fine— except for my father. He adored my mother, and so Elizabeth saw her chance and talked him into rigging the explosion that killed Philip. That way they could each get the person they wanted. Father set up some dynamite in the hanging wall of the Grubstake tunnel and then strung a trip wire across the tunnel. It was a Sunday and Elizabeth persuaded Philip to take Geoffrey hunting in Rob Roy. She knew he would use the Stair. Everything went according to plan, except that Geoff didn't get killed in the cave-in. He was always there to remind her of Philip and of what she'd done. She hated him even more for that.

"Things were fine for Elizabeth for years. But for my father, it was different. My mother became ill and he needed money to pay her medical bills. King offered to loan it to him. He had to take it, but he became obsessed with paying it back. He decided he could make a strike on Cottonwood. It was an idea he and Philip had toyed with briefly. Philip owned the land. Father blackmailed Elizabeth into giving it to him. For her it was a simple price to pay for his silence. She managed to destroy all the old records and deeds that pertained to Philip, and Father then turned up with a deed to be registered. After my mother died, paying King back became an obsession with him. He looked for years on Cottonwood and, of course, found nothing.

"Three years ago everything came to a head. He finally admitted defeat on Cottonwood. When King gave him five per cent of the Cabot stock he couldn't live with his guilt any longer. He decided to disappear, go somewhere and start a new life. He was very careful about setting everything up. He wrote a will that left everything to Geoff if I couldn't be located. He gave Paul his power of attorney just in case any action needed to be taken while the law was waiting to declare him dead. Then he arranged to meet with King so he could tell him the truth.

"But Father was a weak man. He couldn't go through with facing King in the end, so he wrote a confession. Over the years he and King had kept up parts of the Mithral Stair as a memorial to Philip. Father drove his jeep into Mithral Basin and came down the Stair to the library, intending to leave the confession in King's office. Elizabeth was in the library when he came off the Stair. She found out what he was going to do. They quarreled—she tried to talk him out of it. Sometime during their argument Lynn came by and overheard part of it. Finally, Elizabeth pulled a revolver out of the desk drawer, and when Father realized she would kill him, he tried to escape on the Stair. She followed him and shot him. With his jeep parked in the Basin, everyone assumed he'd disappeared into the mountains—just as he'd intended.

"The only flaw in the murder was that Lynn, passing by the library door again, saw Elizabeth come out of the Stair with the revolver. She put things together and concluded what had happened, but she had no proof so she kept silent and spent the next three years watching Elizabeth.

"Nothing happened until King changed his will. Elizabeth hated Geoff so by now that she couldn't stand to see his son have the money she had killed twice for. She thought that if she arranged for Christopher to die in an 'accident,' King would change the will back to Bruce.

"Then I came and started asking questions about my father, the land on Cottonwood. Everything started to unravel. She switched her attention from Christopher to me. She went through the Stair and tried to push me over Rob Roy Falls. When that didn't work, she tried to shoot me—only Bruce stepped in front of the bullet. I think she was totally unstable at the last. She'd doted on Bruce so. Killing him, even accidentally, was more than she could take. But she was still clever. She wanted to get rid of me, but in a way that wouldn't arouse suspicions. She still hoped to get away with it all.

"For my part, I began piecing together what had happened to my father and why, but I never could figure out who was the killer. I knew Lynn knew, but she was trying to protect Elizabeth and wouldn't help me. Then this morning I finally figured it out. I knew that if I could find the clothes Elizabeth wore on her attempts and Christopher's saddle, with the cut cinch, on the Stair, I would have the proof I needed to convince King of what had been happening. I tried to cover myself by calling Angus, but Elizabeth was listening in. She saw her chance and came after me. The rest you know.

"She was a complex woman," I finished. "She wanted money and the power that comes with it. When she had it, she was gracious, lovely, charming—all those things we loved her for. When she didn't have it, or when it was threatened . . ." I held up my hands in a gesture of hopelessness.

No one spoke for a long while. Don Mason arrived with the coroner from Telluride and Geoff and Lynn began making arrangements. I slipped away and went back to the library. I began picking up the books, arranging them in neat piles along the wall. It was the least I could do to help the Cabots set their house in order. I had been there about an hour when Geoff came into the room.

"I've been looking for you." The blue eyes I had once found so icy were staring at me, commanding me in a very compelling way that I found I didn't really mind at all.

"How's King?"

"Don's given him a sedative. It'll take a lot of time for him to recover, I'm afraid. He loved her very much."

I nodded absently. "And Lynn?"

"She's with Paul. She'll come through it. It's been hell on her. No wonder she changed so much, but she's the most resilient of any of us. Paul's a good man. They'll be all right." Then it was his turn to ask a question, one which surprised me. "Where's Christopher? I can't find him."

"I sent him down to Angus. I thought he should be spared that grisly scene of Elizabeth. It's better if he remembers her the way she was. Eventually, he'll have to be told some of the facts, but not today."

"You're very thoughtful." He crossed the room to where I was standing, put his hands on either side of my face, framing it, and looked at me for a long time. I saw him swallow several times. "I thought for a while up there that I'd lost you." He stopped. "This may seem like a bad time, Jenny, but it can't wait. I love you. That's a hard thing for me to say. I've fought against it, tried to run away from it, tried to ignore it. After Nancy I told myself I wasn't going to care for anyone again, but you wouldn't go away. I've been hostile to you, nasty to you, sometimes even cruel to you. I've hurt you, I know that. But after today . . ." He couldn't finish the sentence.

Slowly, he drew my face toward his and then our lips met in a long, tender embrace. He held me close and I could feel the anguish and bitterness seeping away. "I love you, Jenny," he said again. "Will you stay with us—Christopher and me?"

"Yes," I told him calmly. "I'll stay."

This time his embrace was more passionate.